SOMETIMES THE BOOGEYMAN IS REAL

J.E. Daniels

Carpenter's Son Publishing

Sometimes the Boogeyman is Real

© 2022 by J.E. Daniels

Published by Carpenter's Son Publishing, Franklin, Tennessee

Published in association with Larry Carpenter of
Christian Book Services, LLC
www.christianbookservices.com

Cover and Interior Design by Suzanne Lawing

Edited by Anne Tatlock

Printed in the United States of America

978-1-954437-46-3

CONTENTS

Preface

Who are you? Finding out is the greatest mystery you will ever solve, the only question you can solely answer. Many a person enters the grave never really knowing. The mystery of who they are remains unresolved, whether because the person lacked interest, squandered time, or feared the results. This is the cruelest irony of all when the dirt begins to fall.

Don't let it happen to you—

Gretchen's mundane life will soon be riddled
with mystery, murder, and betrayal.
She never fathomed her dreams, and her nightmares,
would be coming true.

Chapter One

WIND AND THE WILL—OH!

"Look, you wormy little toad, who do you think you are? How dare you." Gretchen flings the folder in her hand onto Lloyd's desk. Papers outlining her lousy assignments slide across the polished wood, racing to the edge. She fights the knot swelling in her gut and tries to make her slightly chunky frame stop trembling. Having started her long-suppressed tirade, she cannot back down now. She has been stepped on one too many times and is not taking it anymore.

Thirty-five-year-old Gretchen Crandall has for years rehearsed her confrontation with Lloyd almost nightly before falling asleep. Somehow, now it is happening. She is finding her voice and mustering courage she has never experienced as she stands in Lloyd's office. Why now? What is causing this? She does not know, but she loves every syllable finally reaching Lloyd's ears. Her stomach acid churns and wells up in her throat.

Lloyd snickers in his usual condescending manner. "Whoa! Don't get so bent out of shape. That's a fair deal."

Gretchen stares at Lloyd's perfectly arranged mahogany furniture and the classic blue-gray walls outlining his disheveled silver hair. She grits her teeth and clenches her fists. She hopes her bra absorbs the sweat dripping from her armpits so that it won't show on her new blouse.

"Fair, you say? Fair? Right. Being everyone's *go-for* the ten-and-a-half years it took me to get through college wasn't so bad. I had the hope of becoming a real reporter, but I've had that carrot dangling in front of me too long. It's been nearly six years since I got my degree, and I'm still just a glorified secretary, a token female reporter to make this newspaper appear more liberal.

"Oh, occasionally, I get to cover a social luncheon or fashion debut. But the most interesting information I've reported is lipstick stains dulling the sparkle of the gold lamé on a three-hundred-thousand-dollar designer original. And you even had the audacity to delete that section from my copy." Gretchen hits the back of the chair with her fist, emphasizing her frustration.

Lloyd shakes his head and grins sarcastically.

"Listen, Gretchen; you have been here a long time. But the years you refer to as being a *go-for,* you've generally been leaving around five p.m."

"Well," Gretchen interrupts.

"Hear me out," Lloyd says. "I know there are times you work through the night. That, however, is the exception. So, you haven't *paid your dues* as much as you think you have.

"As I said, there are only two ways to make it. You either *pay your dues,* step-by-step, day-by-day, year-by-year, grind-by-grind. Or somehow, some way, you come up with something spectacular—information that only you have. I suggested interviewing your good-deed-doing, helping-others-promoting, majorly rich hero, Chad Fitzgerald, so that you'd understand the impossibility of shortcuts nowadays. There are those who see him as a saint. But now, he's an inaccessible saint. Although, not everybody buys into his routine. The one thing he is for sure is unreachable." Lloyd's smile widens, and he smirks.

Tapping her pen against her jawbone, Gretchen pauses. "I see. Now I'm supposed to quietly and gratefully return to my old station and burn even more midnight oil on the basket-weaving contest. I'm not asking for an editorial column, just a decent assignment! You say I haven't *paid my dues.* Well, I've done a lot more than Hamer or Don, and they get good assignments."

Squeezing her fist around her pen, Gretchen slides the pen top back and forth as she chews her lip. She takes a slow, deep breath, the way she has practiced.

Gretchen looks Lloyd directly in the eye as she struggles to keep down her lunch. "I'm holding you to what you said. I'm going to get that interview with Chad Fitzgerald, and that gives me the first pick of assignments for three years."

Lloyd laughs. "Gretchen, let's get real here. You'll never get that interview. The biggest and the best have been trying for years. Ever since his highfalutin, socialite wife died, no reporter has gotten anywhere near him. He's become a total recluse. Forget it. Save yourself the heartache."

"I think I'd prefer one huge heartbreak than to have it chipped away a piece at a time. Besides, I have one up on the biggest and best. I'm the most desperate! Fitzgerald is mine."

Lloyd shakes his head again, a habit he developed to give him more time to construct his responses. "Kid, don't do it. You're wasting your time, your energy, and your enthusiasm."

"Funny. That's exactly how I feel about basket weaving," Gretchen replies.

"You're young. You're impatient. You'll never get that interview, and I will repeatedly say, 'I told you so,'" Lloyd nods.

Folding her arms, Gretchen is emphatic. Her satin sleeves make a swooshing noise as they rub against one another, accentuating her resolve.

"You won't get the chance. I'd like to start my long overdue vacation. I have three weeks coming," Gretchen says.

Lloyd inwardly is impressed with Gretchen's newfound courage, although he would never tell her that.

"Of course, you do. As soon as you turn in your current assignments, you can start your vacation. It'll be good for you," Lloyd winks. "Take a nice rest."

"All final copies will be completed by next week." Gretchen starts to leave and turns back. "To be followed shortly by the Fitzgerald interview."

"Yeah, right," Lloyd says.

Gretchen storms out of the office, slamming the door shut. It rattles the plaque beside Lloyd's door frame that reads; *The Pen is Mightier than the Sword, Thomas Jefferson.* Gretchen leans back against the bold writing on the door stating *The NoVa News,* Serving All of Northern Virginia, B. J. Lloyd, Editor-in-Chief. She slaps her palm against her forehead. A hush creeps across the newsroom like a fog. Gretchen scans the faces staring at her. Then she huffs over to her desk, plops in her chair, and pounds away at her computer keys.

Phyllis, Gretchen's shocked co-worker, walks over with her mouth agape. "Wow, girlfriend! That new red blouse sure put some fire in your belly."

"I think it's more from years of garbage, especially from guys. And Lloyd's at the top of the list. I've had it. I'm sick of his nonsense," Gretchen replies. She is the newspaper's only female reporter. All the other females have secretarial or proofreading positions.

Gretchen has been there a long time. She started when she was only nineteen, while she was going part-time to college. With limited funds and always having to work, she could never go to school full-time. Lloyd had promised her a reporter position after she graduated. At least he had kept that promise.

Phyllis nods her head. "Yeah, but like the rest of us, you've been complaining about Lloyd for years. Complaining to us and telling him are completely different. I wanted to applaud, but I need my job. I like our small paper. I'd get swallowed up in one of those big newspapers with a ton of staff. Can you believe *The Washington Post* actually has a thousand reporters? I still can't fathom that the Graham family sold the *Post* to Amazon's Jeff Bezos. Oh well, who could turn down two-hundred-fifty-million dollars?" Phyllis chuckles.

Gretchen stabs her letter opener into her desk, knocking out a small chunk of wood.

"Ooops," she says. "Could you hear what we were saying?"

"Just volume, not the words." Suddenly Phyllis pauses and flares her hands into the air. "Where'd that come from in

Lloyd's office? Is this the same girl who stood silently with her mouth just hanging open while watching your cheating husband and his new girlfriend walk out of the house with your jewelry! I think you've got some pent-up anger bubbling over. You didn't get taken over by an alien or something, did you? Good thing I don't believe in that stuff."

"Honestly, I'm not sure where it came from, but it felt good," Gretchen admits and pushes her keyboard back. "Last night may have played a part. My blind date stood me up; either that or he took one look and ran."

"Girl, will you stop. Look at your beautiful eyes. And face. You are pretty. And your gorgeous, long, brown hair. You just had a lousy mother who did a number on you. I wish you could see what the rest of us do," Phyllis points at Gretchen. "You'll never know who you are until you're willing to see *all* the candid truth about those who have been closest to you in your life. That's when you get to know the real you.

"That mother of yours made your childhood hard and miserable! She did a number on you. But don't give her control of your adult life so she can ruin that, too. Park that baggage in the suitcase closet and refuse to carry it around. Happiness is a choice, and it starts with recognizing and facing your garbage. And you've had a lot of that."

Gretchen points back at Phyllis. "You sound like my Gramma. And you're sweet, no matter how tough you act." She gives her charming half-grin. "You're so right, but that's hard to do."

"Well, you've got to start somewhere," Phyllis says.

"Seriously, I never should've agreed to go on that date. I used to think my jerk ex-husband was in the minority. But after dealing with so many male idiots, I know the males that are slime completely outnumber any good ones."

"Way to avoid the subject again. Maybe the guy got a flat tire," Phyllis ventures.

"I have a cell phone," Gretchen says with a sneer.

"Do you still have a job?" Phyllis asks.

"Yes, and a challenge. Somehow, I've got to make this work," Gretchen says.

"Well, I'm proud of you," Phyllis admits.

"I hope my Gramma is. She was strong. She always told me to speak up. She made me feel like I mattered and what I said counted." Gretchen tilts her head to the side. "But Mom always told me to keep my mouth shut—between lifting the glass to her lips, that is. Or just flat out ignored me," She pauses. "I wish I could've spent more time with Gramma."

Gretchen attempts to lighten the moment. "Also, I wish I wasn't carrying around this extra twenty-three pounds."

"Oh, you look fine. Lighten up," Phyllis replies. "There are too many female skeletons walking around anyway. One day, a big wind's gonna blow them all away. Besides, my husband says most guys like to have some meat on the bones. He says skinny girls feel like the hot buffalo wings when you're done eating them, not good for anything but tossing away," Phyllis laughs her contagious laugh. It always puts Gretchen in a better mood.

Barney, the bald, potbellied newsroom gossipmonger, slips into Lloyd's office. "What's happening? It was sure loud in here, but I couldn't understand what you guys were saying. Is Gretchen getting fired?" Barney asks.

"Fired up, maybe," Lloyd replies. "Women! You try to save them headaches, and they just get defensive. Gretchen will be chopped liver when Fitzgerald gets through with her. But I have to admit I like seeing her with more spunk. I didn't think she had it in her. We'll see if it lasts."

Chapter Two

Desperate Measures

Gretchen works feverishly through the week, mostly at home in her apartment in the Maryland suburbs of Washington, D.C. This way, she does not lose time getting into office conversations. She is on a tight deadline. Her friend and next-door neighbor, Simon, brings her food and makes sure she eats, so she can keep working. He knocks and enters.

"Lunch is here. 'Time flies when you're having fun' and even when you're not. Again, why don't you just stop all this nonsense, marry me, and you'll never have to work again? We'll live happily ever after." Simon gives his big, cheesy grin and places the food tray on the table.

"Uh, because you're gay, and I'm not willing to sacrifice my life just to be your cover," Gretchen responds, peering over her reading glasses. "You know I think you're great, even with all your serious issues. And I love you dearly but come on. That might be 'happily ever after' for you, but for me, not so much. Although, not having to work sounds inviting."

Simon scratches his cheek, shrugs his shoulders, and smiles. "Well, I'm not about to give up my inheritance. Having to prove I can take care of myself before I get a dime isn't fun either, but it makes sense. Fortunes are lost faster than they're made. Besides, I think we would make a cute couple. It's good having you around so much now. It gets lonely working on my computer from home all day. Even though that's the job I wanted and got— job recruiter. Online chats just aren't the same as the real thing."

"At least you *like* your job. Well, I like my job, just not my assignments," Gretchen says, placing her glasses on the table. She lifts the corner of the linen cloth covering the tray. "Wow, this smells wonderful. I sure am glad one of your hobbies is cooking. What is it?"

"This is easy but a favorite. It's egg wrapped in a laver, that's seaweed sheets. The trick is to brush the seaweed with Mongolian fire oil and steam to perfection," Simon answers, fixing their plates. "Don't worry; yours is a mild version. I know you can't eat as spicy as I like it. Delicious and healthy for us. It works with hot sesame oil, too."

"Well, it smells a lot better than it sounds. You're fantastic to do all this. I'd never be so far along without your help. And encouragement," Gretchen adds.

"I think it's the good nutrition I'm getting into you. I don't know how you keep alive eating so many sweets," Simon chides.

"Hey, I eat healthy food too. Besides, dark chocolate's good for me," Gretchen replies.

Simon looks at her sternly. "It's good for you by the ounce, not by the pound." They both laugh.

"Hey, guess what? My dad gave me a compliment. Can you believe it?" Simon says.

"What was it?"

"My dad said that for the most part, the rich people live in Virginia, and the smart people live in Maryland. Unless you live in Potomac or the Columbia area in Maryland. Those are rich places. And he's proud of me living in Maryland to save money. You know, because the cost of living is so much less here than Northern Virginia. Although, I would prefer Virginia."

"Well, that is good. Something positive for a change. But why would you prefer Virginia? The traffic is a nightmare. And we get all the good stuff D.C. has to offer—like the Smithsonian, the Kennedy Center, etcetera—without all the cost and two-hour-plus commute times each way."

"Good point. I guess we are smart, huh?"

Day after day, Gretchen stays focused. She attempts to open avenues to get to Chad Fitzgerald between tackling her various assignments. Initially, with the excitement of possibly meeting Fitzgerald, Gretchen lost three pounds. However, facing so many obstacles and dead ends, she has gained them back plus two more.

The next day at the office, a courier enters the newsroom. "Special delivery letter for Ms. Crandall," he calls.

Gretchen rushes to meet him. "That's me." She grabs the envelope from his hand while everyone watches.

He takes it back. "You have to sign first," he says.

Gretchen signs and grabs the envelope again. Eyes wide, she tears it open and enthusiastically reads the contents. Her shoulders immediately droop, and the corners of her mouth nearly reach her collar bone. She drags back to her desk, leaving the courier without a tip.

Phyllis walks to the guy and slips him some one-dollar bills. Chuckling and shaking her head, she goes over to Gretchen.

"What's it say?" she asks sympathetically.

"Undeliverable! Like everything else I've tried. UPS, FedEx, US mail, carrier pigeon, short-wave radio, even flowers," Gretchen replies with a deep sigh.

"What have you heard from the last detective you hired?" Phyllis asks.

"The same thing the others said, and Lloyd! 'It's impossible to get to him.' Although, at least this last guy did try to bribe Fitzgerald's cook. It didn't work, but he tried," Gretchen says.

"What's next?" Phyllis asks.

"I'm down to my last resort—blackmail." Gretchen puts her hand to her face, covering one eye and part of her forehead.

"What?" Phyllis puts her fist on her hip, which untucks her blouse and shows her midriff bulge hanging over her pants. "What are you talking about?" she asks.

Gretchen lowers her voice even further and leans closer to Phyllis. "Remember that jerk Senate photographer I dated over five years ago, Eddy Osbourne? I can't believe it's been that long. The two-thousand-twenties are flying by even faster than the two-thousand-and-teens did," she sighs. "He's the one that halfway through a function would always give this deep sigh. People think it's because he's bored. But I think it's because he never feels like he fits in, no matter how hard he tries. He's the guy that's all enamored with high society. We broke up because I wasn't classy enough or rich."

Phyllis has a blank look, and Gretchen continues, "You know, they tried to pin a murder on him, but he wasn't even in the country at the time."

"Oh yeah, yeah, that's right," Phyllis says, remembering now.

"Well, he got pictures of Senator Vance in his underwear with a female that wasn't his wife—"

"Vance? He's not like that," Phyllis interrupts.

"I know he's not. He's one of the few that isn't. He was very drunk. I think the girl Eddy hired even drugged him; she was setting him up. Vance completely passed out. Eddy was paying her a lot. He was going to use the photos to splash the tabloids and make a name for himself. And a lot of money. Those photos would have ruined Vance's career and marriage. Plus, all the pain for his wife and kids. I tried to talk Eddy out of it, but, of course, Eddy didn't care."

"What happened?" Phyllis asks.

"I stole the memory card out of Eddy's camera."

"What?" Phyllis shrieks.

"Sssshhh," Gretchen says. "I had to. It was so unjust; I couldn't let it happen. You know how it goes. Even if I had told everyone the truth, most people would think that I was the one lying. Once the lie's in print, it's believable."

"Oh, so true," Phyllis says.

"I lost all respect for Eddy that night. I was afraid to break up with him then because I thought he'd figure out what happened. But I stopped trying so hard to look good, and it wasn't long till he dumped me."

"Wow! I'm impressed again.," Phyllis says, clutching her hand to her chest. "I felt so sorry for you when he dumped you. You should have told me then."

"I didn't tell anybody."

"Where are the pics?" Phyllis asks.

"I have the memory card in a safe deposit box. Eddy thought the girl he hired took it. Boy, was he ticked. I felt kind of bad because there are some legitimate pictures on there, too. But then the stuff with him accused of murder started, and he forgot all about it.

"Vance was Chad Fitzgerald's college roommate. I just don't know if I should resort to blackmail or if I even have the guts to do it."

"You've got more courage than I thought you had. You proved that in Lloyd's office. And wow. How gutsy of you taking that memory card. I'm proud of you, *again*," Phyllis admits.

"That outburst with Lloyd surprised me, too. I can *do* things easier than I can speak up. That's for sure. I always mess up under pressure. I could never be on *Jeopardy*. I think of good things to say when it's too late. And even if I do think of something apropos in the moment, I usually can't get the words to come out of my mouth. I was more shocked than Lloyd when I said those things in his office. But I had rehearsed that for years. If I try this, I'll have to talk to Vance! I just know I'll blow it," Gretchen says with a groan.

"Listen, my friend, you've got to do this for all of us. Start practicing if you have to. Right now, this isn't about Vance as much as it's about Lloyd. You can't let Lloyd win! It's already bad enough around here. Crank up your backbone and pretend you're your Grandma," Phyllis says, shaking her finger at Gretchen. "I'll even make the appointment with Vance for you."

"I wish you could go for me," Gretchen replies.

"Don't start. You can do this," Phyllis says emphatically. "Hey, didn't I read that Eddy's engaged to one of those socialites?"

"Yeah, finally. Wendy Monroe's born and bred pedigreed high society. Not great looking but loaded. He sure has been trying to join that club for years. But from what I hear, she's a real wimp, and he treats her shabbily. However, they say she's crazy about him. We'll see if the family lets the marriage take place. Part of me thinks they'll pay him off, or he'll just disappear." Gretchen raises her left eyebrow and makes a slicing motion across her neck with her finger.

Chapter Three

WHAT FEAR LIES HERE?

The grandeur of Washington, D.C. still awes Gretchen. The city houses the Smithsonian, the Kennedy Center, and her favorite monuments. Not to mention the government that protects and sustains the nation created by her beloved founding fathers, the most successful free country on earth. George Washington and John Adams are her two favorite heroes. How will she ever face Senator Vance, one of the few current senators she admires, and threaten him with blackmail?

Gleaming rays of sunlight sparkle brightly on the Capitol dome. Gretchen is stuck on the third step from the bottom. She is usually invigorated by seeing the building. However, today the three-hundred-sixty-five steps, one for each day of the year at the Front West Entrance, seem very daunting. Today is different. She has mixed feelings and much apprehension about this climb.

Since Gretchen is standing up to Lloyd and trying to get the Fitzgerald interview, all the girls are rooting for her.

Reaching into her pocket, she feels the good-luck items each of the girls she is closest with at the office gave her to help. A St. Christopher's medal from Anne, a cross from Katie, a mustard seed encased in acrylic to look like glass from Jill, a Star of David from Ruth, and an American Indian arrowhead from Charlotte all tumble through her fingers. She left the rabbit's foot from Beth in her purse. She thinks that it is too creepy to hold. The horseshoe from Darla is in her apartment. It is too heavy to carry. Even though Gretchen has read several books on near-death experiences, she is unsure what she believes. However, she figures she needs all the help she can get. Phyllis gave her a hug but nothing for her pocket. "You know I don't believe trinkets have power," she declared. Gretchen is by far closer to Phyllis than anyone.

Phyllis does not believe in luck, except in certain games and cards. She believes in action and hard work. When it comes to God, Phyllis is not sure He exists. However, she is also not certain He does not. Phyllis is not old enough to be Gretchen's mother, but she often fills that need. Gretchen trusts Phyllis more than anyone except her grandmother, whom she misses immensely. Only Phyllis knows about the upcoming blackmail attempt.

Some of Gretchen's co-workers have become her family. They spend holidays together and celebrate all the special occasions, especially birthdays. She loves these people. The truth be known, she even loves Lloyd.

When Gretchen first started working at *The NoVa News*, Lloyd took her to the Library of Congress at the Thomas Jefferson Building. He taught her a love of books she had never known—the feel of the pages beneath her fingertips, the pungent scent of the ink, the glide of the cover, and the strength of the spine, particularly those that are Smyth sewn. These are all things she had never noticed about books before Lloyd.

"There is more to a book than just the story," Lloyd would say. "A good book should become a part of you. It should make you think. It should make you feel. It should challenge you. It should help mold you. It should help you grow. Hold it, feel it, smell it, caress it into your heart and make it part of your soul.

"Be careful what you read. Stay away from trash. It slithers into your soul and takes over your life. People say, 'you are what you eat.' Well, I say, you are what you read! And if you read nothing, what does that make you?" The only time Lloyd references a soul is when talking about books. Gretchen is thankful she knows that side of him. Not many people do.

Gretchen has not been to see her mother in over three years. Her mother still lives in South Carolina and is on her sixth marriage. It is so painful for Gretchen to return to that house, once again watching her mother stumble in a stupor. Gretchen always makes sure something arises with work so she cannot make the trip. Often Gretchen thinks it will be easier to go in a few months, but it just gets more challenging. She only talks to her older sister occasionally. They usually just fight, and keeping distance with time and space is less painful. She is glad to have a family created by choice. The only birth family member she ever misses is her grandmother.

They always had grand times together when Gretchen was with her grandmother. She made her feel loved. Everything they shared and did was exceptional. Her grandmother told her many times that Jesus loves her, but Gretchen cannot understand why Jesus would let her grandmother die if He loves her. She needed her grandmother.

Gretchen's grandmother said she would see her again, but Gretchen needed her then and needs her now! Her life got much more difficult after her grandmother was gone. She was her only respite from her mother and the hard part of her life. When her grandmother died, it was at the end of Gretchen's eighth-grade school year. Gretchen had a long way to go to be grown. She still misses her daily. However, she will not think about it now because it makes her too sad.

The point of the arrowhead pokes Gretchen's finger. She takes her hand from her pocket. Gretchen keeps the mustard seed piece in her clenched fist, knowing she needs a miracle. She chews her bottom lip, then pauses.

"Gramma would never bite her lip. She'd just forge ahead," Gretchen says, looking up at the stairs. She rushes upward as if racing for a touchdown. All the while, Gretchen presses the mustard seed, her favorite piece, into her palm. She remembers her Gramma telling her to believe in miracles and about how you could move a mountain with faith just the size of a mustard seed. "You have to believe in miracles to get a miracle," she would say. Gretchen never quite understood what that meant, but this piece reminds her of her grandmother. She misses her terribly.

Making it partway up, she stops to catch her breath. Her heart is pounding. Remembering the first time she ever rode the underground Senate train, she smiles. It was when she was only fourteen. Her friend's brother worked as a Senate page during the summer while home from college. He took them to D.C. She wonders if he ever knew she had a big crush on him.

A lady with a briefcase knocks into Gretchen, never even noticing her. Gretchen looks at her watch and remembers she forgot her transportation pass. So, she cannot take the underground train to the Senate office building.

"Oh, no!" she yells, running back down the steps. Gretchen catches the toe of her right foot on her left heel and promptly tumbles down the stairs. The blows of the step edges remind her of her mother's drunken anger. Lying face down at the bottom on the sparkled concrete expanse, she gives a familiar sigh of relief. It's over, and no bones appear to be broken, though she can feel the scrapes and bruises all over her body. Gretchen is thankful she was less than halfway up the steps when she turned around to go down them.

Several people walk by, not even slowing their pace. Gretchen struggles to push herself up off the sidewalk.

A man stops. "Here. Let me help you," he says, assisting Gretchen to stand.

"I'm okay. Thank you. Except I feel like a klutz," she replies as she dusts off her clothes.

He picks up her purse. "Oh, it happens to all of us sometimes," he says kindly, handing her the bag.

Gretchen sees his wedding ring. "Please tell your wife I said you're a real gentleman. Unfortunately, that's something rare in this town nowadays," she replies.

"Well, thank you. Are you sure you're okay?" the thoughtful stranger asks.

"Yes. Thanks again," Gretchen says, picking up the mustard seed piece and placing it back in her pocket.

"Have a good day," he says, walking away.

"You too."

Gretchen hurries to the curb and hails a taxi, even though she only has a few blocks to go. She is in no mood to walk, and time is running short. Entering the cab, she notices her ripped stockings.

"To the Russell Senate Office Building, please," she says, sitting down and removing her stockings. She stuffs them in the ashtray as much as she can. "I hate hose anyway," she mutters to herself. "No wonder guys don't wear these things. They're miserable."

Shortly, Gretchen is standing at Vance's office door seven minutes before her appointment. She paces the hall and bites her lip. "Not again," she says, taking her cell phone from her purse and texting her own number. "Note to self: Don't chew your face. It gets swollen and ugly! Forge ahead. Think Gramma."

The door opens, and Gretchen jumps. Two men exit the office. Gretchen grabs the door before it closes and enters.

"Are you Ms. Crandall?" the secretary asks.

"Yes, I am," she says.

"Go on in. Senator Vance is expecting you."

With each step, the lump in Gretchen's throat grows larger. She grabs all five items in her pocket and opens the door with her left hand. "Gramma, here we go," she whispers.

Vance is slightly balding with a large stomach that he hides well with his suit jacket. He is shorter than Gretchen realized and barely reaches five-foot-five-inches tall.

"Hello, Senator Vance. Thank you for meeting with me," Gretchen says as she enters with her hand extended. They shake hands.

"Have a seat, Ms. Crandall," Vance says, motioning to the chair in front of his desk. "Always happy to help the press."

Inwardly, Gretchen is terrified but gets straight to the point. "I need you to arrange for me to interview your college roommate, Chad Fitzgerald."

"Yes, you and every reporter in the country would like that. But Chad gives no interviews," Vance smiles.

Gretchen is wringing her hands behind her purse and trying not to vomit. She clearly explains everything to Vance. Once he finally grasps what had happened with the photos Eddy Osbourne took and what is happening now, Vance is livid.

"You do realize that blackmail is illegal!" he shouts. "You can be arrested."

"Don't think of this as blackmail. Don't even use that word," Gretchen says. "I did you a big favor in taking the photos away from Eddy, and I'm just asking for a favor in return. A favor for a favor, that's all it is."

"A favor I wouldn't even consider if you weren't holding me hostage with those photos!" he says through gritted teeth. "I don't think Chad will give you an interview no matter what I say."

Gretchen takes a business card from her purse and places it on Vance's desk. "Think about the entire situation. You know how to reach me. Everything will seem very fair when you consider all aspects." She stands and walks to the door. "I'll expect to hear from you by five o'clock tomorrow." She leaves his office.

The secretary is gone. Gretchen is relieved. She was surprised she had not come in when Vance started yelling.

Gretchen walks down the hall to the bathroom and immediately loses her breakfast. She goes home, gets in bed with the covers over her head, and goes to sleep. It is easy to sleep since she was up most of the night rehearsing.

Two hours later, Gretchen's cell phone rings. It's Phyllis.

"Are you in jail? Do I need to get a lawyer or bail you out?" Phyllis asks.

"I'm in bed," Gretchen says.

"With Vance?" Phyllis asks.

"Are you nuts? Of course not; I'm home."

"I'm sick with worry because I haven't heard from you, and you're taking a nap! Are you serious? You couldn't call me first?" Phyllis says with anger and hurt.

"I'm sorry. You're right; I should have called. I meant to."

They both feel better after soothing Phyllis's hurt feelings and filling her in on everything that happened. Gretchen hates hurting anyone, especially someone she cares about so much. Phyllis has become the sister she always wished she had.

"You should work from home the rest of the day," Phyllis insists. "I'll get your calls. If Vance calls, I'll forward it to you."

That was an offer Gretchen could not refuse. She pulls the covers back over her head and sleeps until evening. She eats and goes back to bed, sleeping until her clock's alarm rings the following morning. The phone never rang.

Chapter Four

PERILS AND PANIC

The next day goes as usual, except for Phyllis and Gretchen exchanging shrugs and eye queries more frequently. There is still no word from Vance. By two-thirty, Gretchen cannot stop watching the clock. She carries papers to Phyllis's desk.

"I can't take it anymore. What if I don't hear from Vance? What if he blows me off?" Gretchen asks.

Phyllis moves closer. "Don't panic yet. You gave him till five o'clock. And I've been thinking about that. If you don't hear from him, you've got to print out one of the pictures and take it to him to see. Don't give it to him. That'll give him evidence to press charges. But let him see how bad it looks. He'll come around then," she says, nodding her head confidently.

"I guess you're right. I just don't know if I can go through meeting with Vance again. I hope he calls," Gretchen confesses with a sigh.

The phone rings. They both scramble to get it. It is for Phyllis.

Gretchen tries to work but cannot think about anything but Vance. She makes a trip to the snack machine and gets pretzels. The bags are small, and it is empty in ninety seconds. No help there. She goes to the candy machine and gets chocolate. She tries to savor it, but it disappears in three gulps. There was no help there, either. She knows she is in big trouble now. Chocolate always works. She looks at the clock; it's four-thirty-five. She hates the idea of having to meet with Vance again. The thought crosses her mind that she wants a drink. However, after living through those years with her mother, that is one idea she never allows to linger.

A man in a sheriff's uniform with a badge enters the newsroom. "Ms. Crandall? Ms. Gretchen Crandall?" he calls.

Gretchen and Phyllis look at each other. Gretchen falls to her knees and grabs the trashcan. Just as she is about to lose her now chocolate-covered pretzels, Phyllis reaches her desk and hands her a tissue.

"Get up! *Now!*" Phyllis demands, pulling on Gretchen's arm. "You're looking guilty as sin. Right now, it's just his word against yours, and you can plead the fifth. Don't blow this."

"I don't want to go to jail," Gretchen says.

Gretchen sits back in her chair and takes a drink of water. The officer repeats her name, and everyone looks her way. Phyllis places her hand on Gretchen's shoulder.

"Oh, that's me," Gretchen says with a wave.

The officer walks to her desk. "Gretchen Crandall?"

"Yes," she responds. Gretchen is now as white as the paper in her printer.

Phyllis interrupts and extends her hand. "Hi, I'm Phyllis Gower."

The officer ignores Phyllis. "Ms. Crandall, Senator Vance…."

Gretchen grabs her stomach with her left hand and flails her right hand, knocking over her glass of water. Liquid runs everywhere, including into Gretchen's lap. She quickly stands. Phyllis grabs tissues and dabs the papers.

The officer puts up his hands and says, "This looks like a bad time. Do you want me to come back later?"

Phyllis and Gretchen both freeze. Finally, they look at each other and then at the officer.

"What?" Gretchen asks, sitting back down in her chair.

"Do you want me to come back?" he asks.

"No, uh no," Gretchen says. "Now is fine."

The officer reaches into his pocket and takes out an envelope. He holds it out toward Gretchen. "Senator Vance asked me to bring this to you."

Gretchen looks silently at the envelope. "What's this about?" she asks.

The officer shrugs. "My job is just delivery, not to know what it says."

Gretchen stares at the officer, then asks, "So you're not going to arrest me?"

"Arrest you?" The officer looks puzzled. "Why? Have you done something wrong?"

"Oh no! No, of course not. I just—"

"Well, do you want this envelope or not?"

"Yes. Yes, of course."

As she takes the envelope, Gretchen and Phyllis burst out laughing. They cannot stop.

Gretchen is nodding her head and gesturing with her hand. She laughs so hard she cannot speak. Tears stream down

Gretchen's cheeks. The laughter is such a release from the tension of the day.

The officer is perplexed and looks at them as if they are crazy. He backs up slowly.

Still laughing, Phyllis manages to say, "Sorry. Inside joke."

The officer leaves, shaking his head. Everyone is looking at Phyllis and Gretchen.

"Oh, get back to work," Phyllis says. "Haven't you ever seen two women laugh before?"

By this time, Gretchen is taking deep breaths and calming down somewhat. "I have never been so scared or so relieved in my life."

"Me either. I thought for sure the sheriff was here to arrest you. Whew." Phyllis puts her hand on her head. "Well, open it."

Gretchen does just that. She rips open the envelope and pulls out a note and a fancy plastic card. The card says Kings Landing Boat Dock Pass with eight numbers. She reads the message.

"Crandall, Meet me at the boat dock at 1:30 pm next Thursday. It's close to Jekyll Island, GA. I cannot make any promises, but I will try. *Don't be late.*"

Gretchen and Phyllis grab hands and jump up and down together. Phyllis is saying, "You did it! You did it." And Gretchen is saying, "We did it! We did it."

Barney looks at Don. "Somebody must be getting married. Females. I just don't understand them."

Chapter Five

BAGS PACKED AND PUFFY

Thursday finally arrives. After slaving over her office keyboard all night, Gretchen's last assignment covering the fifth-grade essay contest is finally complete. Lloyd always likes including events about kids and teens to keep parents and grandparents subscribing to the paper. Now she tries to rewrite what she will say to Fitzgerald.

"Good morning, Gretchen. You sure are here early," Anne, one of the proofreaders, says and starts making fresh coffee.

"Actually, I'm here late," Gretchen replies. She yawns and stretches. She is exhausted.

"Well, looking closer, I can see that." Anne smiles. "What are you doing?"

"I've been desperately searching for the right words, the correct phrases, the key of acceptance. My whole future is hanging by my powers of persuasion condensed into a paragraph. It has to work; I've plotted and prepared all week. This plan is the way out of my perpetual rut," Gretchen sighs.

Anne is puzzled. "Have you lost it? Are you okay?" she asks.

Gretchen jumps up and grabs Anne's arm. "Now is my chance, my escape project, my first step toward the Pulitzer Prize. I'll show Lloyd!"

Anne pats Gretchen's shoulder. "Honey, if you're showing up Lloyd, I'm all for it. But right now, I think you could use a cup of coffee. Decaf, that is."

"I don't have time. I'm packed, have my ticket, and going to the beautiful south. Georgia, here I come. But don't let Lloyd know anything. He knows I'm taking my vacation but nothing else. I don't want him putting obstacles in my way. There're enough of those already." Gretchen gathers her papers and files as she talks. "I'll call you. I will need access to info as I go along but don't let anyone know it's me calling. Okay?"

"Sure," Anne shrugs her shoulder. "You can count on me to keep it all quiet."

"Thanks. You're a doll. I'm off." Gretchen puts a box and a note on Phyllis's desk and hurries out of the newsroom.

"Good luck," Anne yells. "Or is that break a leg?" she mutters. "Sometimes, I think I'm the only sane person in this place."

Sitting on the plane waiting for take-off, Gretchen thinks in awe, *I can't believe I'm doing this. I never thought it would work this far. Senator Vance will meet me at the boat dock, although he could've let me fly in his plane. No, that would've raised questions.*

Gretchen thinks. *Well, it looks like I have two things over 'the biggest and the best' –desperation and Eddy's photographs. That lousy, no-good…uh! Why can't I think of a word to call a guy that doesn't reflect on his mother?*

"Would you like a pillow?" the flight attendant asks.

"Yes, please. With the way I look, it's obvious why you offered me a pillow. Do I get charged extra for the bags under my eyes?" Gretchen laughs.

Gretchen gets as comfortable as possible in the upright position. She places her pillow against the side of the plane behind the window for a nice view but immediately falls asleep. Exhausted, Gretchen does not awaken until the flight attendant brings the meal. She requests an extra lemon. Gretchen eats only a little. Then she bites a lemon slice in half and places the cold half slices under her eyes on the puffiness. She reclines and goes back to sleep.

As the plane readies to land, Gretchen does not stir. Drool has dripped out of the side of her mouth and onto her jacket. The flight attendant gently nudges her shoulder.

"Ms., Ms., we're preparing for landing. Please bring up your seat and—"

Gretchen awakes with a start. "Oh, yes. Of course." She wipes her mouth with the back of her hand and prepares for landing.

Once on the ground, she scurries to the baggage conveyor belt, gets her luggage, and then grabs a sandwich. She takes the shuttle to her hotel and checks in to her reserved room. Her nerves and insecurities battle her every movement. However, she does not have time to give in to either of them. She dons her best outfit and calls the front desk requesting a taxi.

Rushing to the lobby, she forces herself to breathe slowly and attempt to relax. She sits on the outside bench and refreshes her mascara until the cab arrives. Barely giving the driver time to stop, she hurries into the backseat of the cab.

"Where to?" the driver asks. "It sure is a pretty day to be goin' anywhere."

"The Kings Landing Boat Marina, as quickly as possible, please," Gretchen answers.

The driver pulls away. "Consider it done. But I can only take you as far as the security gate. It's hard to get in that place. They're real persnickety about who's who and what's what."

"So I've heard. But today's my lucky day; I have a pass," Gretchen says.

"Well, Miss, you be sure and hold onto that pass, 'cause they just love arrestin' people around here, especially a pretty little thing like you. You just better watch out."

"I can take care of myself quite well, thank you," Gretchen huffs and tries to act offended. She hates to admit she liked being called pretty and little. It makes her extra pounds seem less intimidating.

"No offense intended. Just a friendly warnin'," the taxi driver replies. "It's not far to the marina. We'll be there soon."

They pass large, gorgeous homes, one after the other. Each has a vast, manicured lawn, and many have sprinklers running. Gretchen wonders why no children are playing in the sprinklers or anywhere. She assumes the children must be in the back yards, behind the fences. She remembers playing freeze tag growing up with the neighborhood kids. It was fun, and it was a relief to be out of her house.

As they reach the security gate, the guard stops the taxi. "Sorry. No entry here," he says.

"I'm just dropping her off, and she has a pass," the driver replies.

The guard looks at Gretchen. "What's your name? And I'll need your pass and a photo ID."

"Crandall. Gretchen Crandall," she says, handing him her pass and driver's license. "It should be listed under Senator Vance."

"Yeah, it's here. Just step through the metal detector and have a seat on the bench. A transport will be by to pick you up in a few moments," the guard says, opening the door and handing her back her ID. "Senator Vance has slip fifty-three."

Gretchen pays the driver and walks through the archway toward the bench. The guard says something she cannot hear into his radio, then stops her.

"Sorry, but you will have to leave the camera and picture-taking cell phone here with me," he says.

Gretchen is stunned. "But what if I get a call."

"You can't get a call on the island where you're registered to go. There's no cell reception, and Mr. Fitzgerald likes it that way. This is your claim check. You can retrieve your items upon departure from Kings Landing."

Gretchen wants to object but recognizes the futility of even trying; she hands over the articles and sits on the bench. A sign indicates the private airport in one direction and the private marina the opposite way. Momentarily, the transport arrives, which is nothing more than a golf cart with fancy lettering.

A teenage boy jumps out and asks, "Gretchen Crandall for slip fifty-three?"

"Yes," she answers and gets in the golf cart.

Gretchen stares at every yacht they pass as they make their way down the dock. She sees people lounging on decks, being catered to by maids. Gretchen knows she relates more to the maids than to anyone else she sees here.

As they approach slip fifty-three, Vance is standing in a speedboat tied to his yacht. "You're late. Hurry up," he shouts.

"Five minutes. I'm sorry," Gretchen replies, walking to the boat.

Before Gretchen steps into the boat, a man at the dock approaches her. "Excuse me, but you have to empty your purse on this table before you leave," he says, pointing the way.

"Really?" she asks.

"Hurry up, Crandall," Vance says sternly.

Gretchen dumps the contents of her purse and spreads the articles across the table with her hand. "Satisfied?" she asks.

The man places the items individually back in her purse. He tries to open the rabbit's foot, thinking it's hiding something. Then he runs it over a magnetic field to be safe. Saving face, he comes to a plastic travel tampon holder and opens it. Inside is a tiny camera, which he keeps.

"That's been tried before," he says, handing the purse back to Gretchen. He offers his hand to help her into the boat and gives her a life jacket. "Have a nice day."

Gretchen sits on the seat nearest the step. She is embarrassed and, at this moment, does not mind Vance's silence.

"Are you ready to leave, Senator Vance?" the young man at the wheel of the boat asks.

Vance nods.

"Please fasten your life jackets, and we're off," the young man says.

The boat gently glides over the water as if it has wings. The wind feels wonderful on Gretchen's face. She likes watching the waves the speed creates, melting all the way to the land on either side.

Now Gretchen wishes Vance would at least say something to her. Yelling over the grind of the speedboat engine, she attempts to soften Vance's hostility.

"We must be getting closer. I've seen several gigantic *no trespassing* signs," Gretchen says.

Vance glares at Gretchen coldly and offers no response.

"Senator Vance, please don't think of this as blackmail. Just consider it leverage. Like we discussed, just a favor for a favor. I need to get an interview with Chad Fitzgerald. For the past almost five years, he's been in seclusion, and you're the only non-relative that's seen him. I've tried everything else I could think of—letters, phone calls, telegrams, even short-wave radio—but nothing's worked. I'm only asking that you talk him into letting me have a short exclusive."

"'Asking,' Ms. Crandall? 'Asking,' you call it? Those photographs could ruin my career and my marriage!" Vance snaps.

"Would you have listened to me otherwise?" Gretchen asks.

"Probably not, but I don't think anything I say will persuade Chad to go public, not even for just one article."

"You'll think of something," she says.

Gretchen dramatically turns to climax the conversation. She does not want to reveal that she would never use the outdated material to destroy a man's life, especially since it was a set-up.

Senator Vance has no way of realizing the despair Gretchen feels. Not only is her biological clock ticking like a bomb, but she also has no career to show for it. How is Vance to know that she had given youthful years putting her ex-husband through college, only to be left for a bottle-blond whose bras size was higher than her I.Q. Gretchen survived that, but the hope and optimism that carried her through the last eight-and-a-half years are wearing thin. She hates resorting to threats but sees no other way.

Hoping her ploy has worked, Gretchen gazes in amazement at the beautiful scenery. There is nothing remotely close to this where she spends her passing days. The lake is an incredible blue, and an abundance of water lilies and cattails caress the length of the shoreline. The inlets are full of enormous, elegant white flowers and lily pads holding frogs. Majestic, emerald-green trees rise shoulder to shoulder, reaching for the sun. In the distance to the west, there is a magnificent skyline of royal mountains exquisitely carved to enhance the radiant sunsets. It is easy to see why Fitzgerald has retreated here.

Wondering what Fitzgerald has done to deserve all this opulence, Gretchen watches the water spray trailing the boat. She enjoys the mist touching her face until she realizes it is dissolving her mascara. The boat begins to slow. Gretchen spots a man with binoculars peering their way. She smiles and waves; to wit, he promptly storms off and vanishes from sight.

"Was that Chad Fitzgerald?" Gretchen asks.

No one responds as the boat nears the ramp. The boat slows as it pulls close to the dock. With the boat still swaying, Senator Vance steps onto the pier.

"Captain, please wait here until I return. Make sure she stays on board," Vance says, pointing to Gretchen.

"Good luck," Gretchen calls.

Vance, once again, ignores her and walks toward the house. Gretchen surveys the area from the boat. It is breathtaking and, indeed, everything she has heard.

There are acres of immaculate greenery, a three-story mansion, and a guesthouse. The tool shed is bigger than the places Gretchen has lived. Over the years, there have been rumors that there are three pools, but none are in view.

Studying the water-fairing cabby Vance has just knighted to *Captain*, Gretchen ponders. She hopes he might be a good source of information, even though he does not look old enough to vote.

"So, what's your name?" Gretchen asks.

"Larry, ma'am."

Gretchen shakes her head and places her hand on her cheek. "Now why is it that when a man is called *sir*, it denotes respect and authority. But somehow, being called *ma'am* makes me want to start counting my crow's feet and wonder why I bother to shave my legs."

"Huh?" Larry asks.

Gretchen chuckles. "Never mind. Have you lived around here long?"

"Yes, ma'am. All my life. I'm a senior at Wilford High."

"Where are you going to college?" Gretchen asks.

"Oh, I'm not. I'm goin' into the family business with my daddy."

"What about your friends?"

"Well, two are coming to work for us, and Bud's working for his uncle."

"Do you plan to travel and see the world or anything first?" Gretchen asks.

"What for? The way I see it, Mr. Fitzgerald has seen the world. Why, from what I hear, he owns half of it. And all he wants to do is be right here," Larry says.

"Well, I guess that's the trouble with being raised in a small community with a close-knit family and terrific friends. You grow up happy and content, with no desire to go out and experience the misery the rest of us live in while trying to find your kind of peace," Gretchen grins.

Larry scratches his head. "You plum lost me, ma'am."

"I'm sorry, Larry. I need a good night's sleep. Is it true that no one ever sees Mr. Fitzgerald, except for the few visitors he allows occasionally?"

"Yeah. Every Monday, a crew comes out to take care of the grounds and do maintenance, but they never see him. On Thursdays, food gets delivered, and they clean the houses, but they don't see him either.

"There's a lady in town who cooks all his meals and fixes them, so he just has to pop them in the microwave. She's the only one he talks to. He gives all his instructions through her."

"What keeps people from just renting a boat and knocking on his door?" Gretchen asks.

"That's easy. Except at specified times, he has killer guard dogs everywhere. Dobermans, you know. You can hear them barking from the pens. A couple of years ago, a few guys from school tried to come over here, and the dogs swam after the boat before they even got to shore. As soon as Mr. Fitzgerald hears the dogs barking, he calls the police, and they come right then. He even supplied the police department with a boat.

"The fellows had to do six months community service for trespassin'. Even though they never reached the land because he owns the water too!" Larry motions with his hand.

"Why doesn't he have any guards—men, I mean?" Gretchen asks.

"He used to, but one of them got caught taking pictures to sell to a tabloid. That's when he got the dogs," Larry says.

"Is that why I couldn't bring my cameras?"

"Yeah! We know how you reporters work—take pictures and apologize later. I'd lose my job and reputation if you got shots. Honor is about the only thing that overrides southern hospitality. Besides, you'd have gotten caught. Everybody does."

"Well, I don't have a camera since your dockhands took them captive, but I would like to look around."

A large boat pulls up to the far dock. People begin unloading supplies.

"Who's that?" Gretchen asks.

"Today's Thursday. Like I said, they deliver food and clean the houses. But not one of them has ever seen Mr. Fitzgerald," Larry says.

"Larry, look at all these people. Please let me go just for five minutes. I can help them carry stuff."

"I couldn't do that," Larry says, shaking his head.

"I'll give you fifty dollars if you let me take a peek. No one will ever know," Gretchen pleads.

"I'll know."

Gretchen stares at the sincerity and innocence dripping from Larry's face. "Oh no, blackmail, now bribery! I'm going down fast. They say that everyone has their price. But when you're working with three hundred in travelers' checks and two credit cards nearly to the limit, it's hard to be convincing. Besides, Larry, I can tell you're Mr. Clean in his puberty stage and won't go astray. The worst thing you'll probably do in life is to have *Mother* tattooed on your chest."

"What are you talking about?" Larry asks.

"As I said, I need sleep. It's been a long week." Gretchen motions to the other boat. "Larry, no one would notice me at all. They would be glad for the help."

"I'm sorry, Miss Crandall, but we have to follow our instructions."

"That's MS!" Gretchen replies in frustration.

Gretchen watches the activity from her floating confinement for hours. Larry would not budge from his guardian stance. Gretchen tries everything, including offering free needlepoint lessons for his mother, but nothing works. Different people journey to and from the boat, carrying everything from toilet paper to shoe polish. She carefully memorizes their features to recognize them in town for questions. Gretchen is thankful the dock hands did not confiscate her binoculars.

As everyone disappears to their respective duties, Gretchen wonders why Fitzgerald would polish his shoes. Who would see them? She figures Fitzgerald either has to be an appearance fanatic or bored to a level of despondency, which she is rapidly reaching.

In an attempt to keep her sanity, Gretchen takes her travel sewing kit from her purse. "Larry, do you mind if I fish?"

"No, ma'am. If you think you can haul in a twenty-pound bass with that string, I'd be proud to watch."

"Guess not, huh? Some poor trout would just end up swimming around with a needle threader stuck in his gut." Gretchen sighs. "Hey, Larry, I've heard Fitzgerald has three swimming pools. Is that true?"

"I don't know. You'd have to ask one of the groundskeepers or dog trainers."

"Good idea."

"Miss…Ms. Crandall, would you mind telling me just how Mr. Fitzgerald got so rich? I've heard all sorts of stories from drugs to bombers."

Gretchen laughs. "He started pretty well off. His dad was a millionaire from his telephone system and railway investments. Fitzgerald inherited all that a few years ago, but he was already wealthy in his own right from his books and plays. And all of his stories promote helping others. He also inherited his wife's fortune when she died. But what makes him so different from most of the rich crowd is how he genuinely cares about people and actually helps them. Quietly, with no fanfare. He's done countless good deeds with no one knowing. I've even had trouble researching them because he wants everything kept so private. Unlike the typical wealthy person, who helps for show."

"Wasn't Mrs. Fitzgerald one of those high society ladies?"

"Yes. Very high society."

They wait in that little speedboat for hours. Gretchen is becoming discouraged. She feels if Vance had successfully persuaded Fitzgerald, he would have summoned her by now. The cleaning crew is even returning to the boat.

"What are they doing?' Gretchen asks.

"Looks like they're finished."

"Are you sure there's no way I can convince you to let me tour the grounds? It means so much to me."

"So does privacy to Mr. Fitzgerald. I'd have to alert the police, like I said before."

"Well, Larry, I have accepted the fact that you are filled to the larynx with honor, and I'm leaving. I'm going to get that supply boat to give me a lift back to town. I'm tired of waiting. Please tell Senator Vance that I'll talk to him later. You're a good kid. Hang in there."

"I'll walk you to the boat," Larry says.

Gretchen smiles. "I thought you just might do that."

Larry helps Gretchen out of the boat and escorts her across the dock to the vessel, preparing to depart. She boards the boat. Larry stands there like a sentinel. She waves to him as they pull away.

"Take care, Larry, and have a terrific life."

"Thanks. You too," Larry yells.

Gretchen hurriedly goes searching for the captain of the boat. His wife is having a baby, and he is not there. Today the boat is being operated by a couple of scruffy wharf rats, Tom and Martin. They are a far cry from Larry. Both are much older and very interested in the idea of being bribed. It is not as though they have lost their honor and ideals over the years; it is more that they never had any. Gretchen sees this as an incredible piece of luck but is unsure which bauble in her purse worked.

These two unsavory characters resent Fitzgerald and his wealth, even though he provides many jobs for the community. They relish the idea of putting one over on him and eagerly take Gretchen's money. Tom says they cannot take her to shore because the others will see. However, when they round the bend out of Larry's sight, one will create a distraction, and the other will help Gretchen slip overboard. She can then swim to Fitzgerald's. Not exactly an ideal entrance, but Gretchen is willing to try anything, including destroying her outfit.

Chapter Six

SINK OR SWIM

Gretchen clips her hair to the top of her head and slips her shoes under her belt. She holds her dress tightly between her knees as Martin lowers her into the beautiful but cold lake. She treads water as quietly as she can, then slowly swims with one arm, holding her purse out of the water with the other arm. Tom keeps the cleaning crew distracted by claiming he spotted a bear, and Martin quickly gets their boat behind a clump of trees, so Gretchen is not in sight.

Gretchen swims. *I can't believe I'm doing this*, she thinks. *I can't believe this is happening. I'll probably wake up at my desk with Lloyd screaming something, only to find this has all been a dream. Nah. If I were dreaming, I would certainly make this water warm. This bribe is the best two hundred dollars I've ever spent. I'll show Lloyd.*

Reaching the small, sandy beach, Gretchen quickly steps out of the water onto the shore.

Oh yuck, she thinks. *Nothing feels worse than wet stockings stuck to your legs, especially covered with sand. I'd rather be eaten by ants. Uh, maybe not. Oh well, it's all for the good of the story, whatever that means.*

Gretchen quickly moves to a group of bushes for cover. *If my calculations are correct and I can snip the phone lines, I'll be alone with Fitzgerald until Monday when the grounds crew comes. What an exclusive. I'm really here! I hope there's something in the tool shed I can use to kill the phones.*

Gretchen moves quickly and quietly toward the house. As they have been all day, the dogs bark continuously from their locked fence barrier. Gretchen reaches the patio and hears Vance shouting at Fitzgerald through the open window of the guest cottage. She steps closer to listen. Gretchen sees Vance standing and Fitzgerald sitting in an over-stuffed brown leather chair through the window. She immediately crouches down under the window to hear but not be seen.

"We've been friends since our freshman year of college, Chad. You've got to give her an interview. Don't you understand? She could ruin me!" Vance pleads. "Besides, ever since Kathleen died, you've shut yourself off from the world. I know how much you loved her and how unexpected her death was, but you can't go on like this. It's been well over four years. Your mourning has turned into hibernation. Kathleen would not want that. You're only forty-six years old, Chad. That's so young to have a self-imposed life sentence of misery."

Gretchen can feel the tension radiating through the walls and expects Fitzgerald to respond in an angry explosion. Quite to her surprise, his rebuttal is emphatic but very stately.

Fitzgerald stands up, walks to the front of the desk, and sits on the corner. "Misery? Yes. Self-imposed? Never! It came with the satin-lined casket and the sweet stench of so many flowers I felt sick.

"If I did want to rejoin the maniacal madness out there, being inspected and dissected by some verbal bloodhound is the last thing I'd choose. No, you're on your own. I'm just sorry you ever did anything to place yourself in this position. A good lesson for not drinking, I'd say."

Gretchen presses herself against the outside wall. Her increased admiration for Fitzgerald overrides the disappointment she feels in Fitzgerald's refusal to see her. Gretchen wants to watch his mannerisms as he has this exchange with Vance. She gingerly moves to the other side of the window and squats by a perfectly trimmed Japanese Holly bush. A loud snap nearly sends Gretchen out of her skin. Her heart is thumping. At first, she thought she broke a stick when she stepped. Then she realized her knee cracked when she bent. Trading agility for wisdom happens to the biggest, the best, and the desperate.

Waiting for the courage to steal a peek, Gretchen inwardly gives Vance credit for pleading his case. He certainly has tried, including admitting his compromising position to Fitzgerald. As Gretchen's heartbeat quietens, her courage surfaces, and she can hear Vance again.

"Please think about it and call me later. Consider Miriam; I don't want to hurt her."

"Frank Vance, you should have considered Miriam before you fell for that girl's flattery. You're not laying that guilt on me. If your wife gets hurt, you have no one to blame but yourself."

"You're right. Well, I'll talk to you later. Please consider it."

Recognizing the beginning of an exit, Gretchen quickly but carefully retreats. Being caught now would be terrible. She hurries down the slope and hides in the cabana next to the pool. Her adrenalin soars.

The cabana is as incredible as the rest of the surroundings. It has rounded stone archways with long sheer curtains and Cleopatra chairs. The floor is made of interlocking brushed slate, so it will not be slippery. Once inside, she can see three pools as she has heard. One is smaller, a diving pool. It is the only one with diving boards. The other two pools are gigantic but identical. Standing there, staring, Gretchen has no idea why they are alike.

That's not very imaginative, she thinks. *For that matter, why are there two identical? Fitzgerald doesn't need the space for parties. What a shame all this is just for one person. It almost seems sinful. However, I guess it wasn't supposed to be for just one.*

She hears Vance and Fitzgerald coming. The soles of their shoes pound against the path and echo in the greenery. Cold, clammy perspiration oozes from her pores. Uncontrollably, Gretchen begins biting her nails, a habit she has conquered until now. Through a crack in the blinds, she sees Fitzgerald walking Vance part way to the dock. To her surprise, Fitzgerald is much better looking than she expected. He has aged to a dashing salt-and-pepper gray that, mixed with his broad shoulders and boyish smile, is not only very distinguished but quite sexy as well.

Watching them saunter down the path talking casually, Gretchen notices Vance gestures a lot as he speaks. They stop for a moment. Then Vance walks out of sight, and Fitzgerald goes toward the main house. Gretchen ducks behind the lounge seat next to the wall.

As soon as Vance and Larry leave, Gretchen knows she and Fitzgerald will be alone. No help lives here any longer since the guys were caught taking pictures to sell to the tabloids. Fitzgerald's attorney is friends with one of the owners of the first tabloid. He figured he would rather score points with Fitzgerald than to print some boring photos. The employees had all signed confidentiality agreements, so they readily handed in everything connected to the photos to avoid legal charges. Now, help only comes at appointed times and leaves immediately after they are done.

Being on the island with Fitzgerald is more than Gretchen ever hoped would happen in all her planning. She wants to achieve an interview, which she counts on to change her career status at the paper. However, a weekend exclusive can change her life.

There have been many attempts by reporters and others to reach Fitzgerald. Usually, people want him to back an invention, finance a business, or donate money to some cause. However, they have all been unsuccessful. Incredibly, Gretchen is standing on his floor, breathing his air and hiding in his cabana.

Gretchen waits breathlessly until the sound of Larry's boat is nearly inaudible. Quickly, she throws away her stockings, rinses off the remaining residue of the sand, and combs her hair. She quietly makes her way to the tool shed and finds a pair of garden shears. Carefully, she sneaks about the estate. Gretchen cuts what she hopes are all the phone lines to each area, including the pools. The garden shears remind her of her grandmother, but she has no time to think right now. She is just winging this entire escapade. Gretchen plans to insist on paying for the repairs. That is a small investment to change her whole future.

Impressed by her courage and ingenuity, Gretchen feels rather proud of herself. No one has ever made it this far, including a hot air balloon attempt. With this shot of confidence, she decides to take the bold approach and knock on the front door. She just knows Fitzgerald will be as impressed with her as she is with herself.

As she walks up the path, the other side of Fitzgerald's mansion comes into view. It is breathtaking. Every window arched, and each facing hand carved. French doors lead to balconies decorated with eighteenth-century furniture and draped with luscious plants. It is such a contrast to Gretchen's bent aluminum patio chairs sitting on broken bricks. Again, she thinks that all this is too much for one person. *How can he possibly use eight balconies?*

The magnificent landscaping everywhere accents the grandeur of the dwelling. Several different tiers lead from the house filled with countless flowers and perfectly positioned marble benches. Five fountains spout musically choreographed water, and all this overlooks a glorious view of the lake. This scenery is the closest thing to paradise Gretchen has ever seen.

Straightening her posture, she steps onto the front veranda amid twenty-foot hand-carved columns, abruptly reminding her of her five-foot-three-and-one-quarter-inch stature. That quarter-inch is important to Gretchen; she has always wanted to be taller. When she was a girl in high school, her height was perfect because she was considered cute and dainty. However, somehow when she became a woman, she felt alluring and glamorous did not come under five-seven.

Suddenly, Gretchen realizes she is overwhelmed by some ridiculous insecurities. *I'm being absurd,* she thinks. *Have I forgotten the basic principles of women's suffrage? You cannot measure quality, ability, and intellect in inches. Nor sex appeal!*

Continuing her pep talk, Gretchen recalls how far she has come and how impressed Fitzgerald will be, not to mention Lloyd. Her dress is a little wrinkled but is drying nicely. It was a bit expensive for her but is designed for travel and easy care. She is pleased with her purchase. Confidently, she walks to the door and firmly knocks. She rehearses modest ways to accept Fitzgerald's adulation. A slight miscalculation; Fitzgerald is livid.

Chad opens the door. "Who are you, and why are you on my property?" Fitzgerald asks brusquely. His expression of incredulity immediately turns to fury.

"Oh, I know who you are," he continues. "You'd better haul tail. The dogs will be out in less than six minutes, and you'll be torn limb from limb, which is what you deserve!"

Fitzgerald tries to slam the door, but Gretchen jams in her purse to stop it. What happened to the praise? Where is the adulation? This response is entirely unexpected. Her optimism had smothered her common sense.

"I can't leave. I don't have a boat."

"You better swim fast then because the dogs will get you in the water if you're close to the shore."

"So I've heard! Don't you even want to know who I am or how I got here?"

"No. I figure you're that blackmailing, low-life leech of a reporter that Frank told me about. You slithered ashore through either intimidation or bribery!"

"Well, it wasn't quite that simple."

"Close enough. Crandall, I believe. Now leave. If you're on this porch when the timer lets the dogs out, they'll rip you to shreds. It's a shame Vance isn't with you! I never thought he'd stoop to this."

"Vance doesn't know I'm here. He had nothing to do with this. But there's no way I can swim back to town. If the dogs don't get me, I'll drown."

"Then I suggest you head for the woods. As long as you're not near the house or the shore, the dogs should leave you alone. Just wait there for the sheriff. It won't be long."

"Yes, it will. I cut all your phone lines. Can't we please just talk?"

"No. First of all, I have electrical tape, and I think I can manage to splice a cord. Secondly, if I fail, there's a radio in my helicopter. You weren't quite as thorough as you thought now, were you? I figure you've got about two minutes of hard running, or you're in serious trouble."

"Couldn't I just wait inside for the sheriff?"

"No. I'm not interested in having my interior described in a late-night copy. About a minute-thirty seconds. Good luck."

Pushing her purse out of the way, Fitzgerald closes the door. Gretchen takes his advice and begins running. She cannot imagine anyone allowing canines to dismember another human, but he does many things she finds hard to fathom. Gretchen decides relying on her athletic ability is wiser than counting on Fitzgerald's charity. She runs faster than she has ever run.

Soon she can hear the ferocious barking drawing closer and knows the dogs are free. Gretchen runs with all her strength, hoping to reach a safe area. Her chest aches, her throat burns, and her legs tremble. She regrets rejecting all those invitations to jog.

With each stride, Gretchen recounts how stupid she has been. She has wasted her vacation, money, and best outfit for nothing. Worse than that, she feels she will have to face the following year with the hope of writing obituaries as her most significant goal.

Mingled through the barking, Gretchen begins hearing a man yelling. It has to be Fitzgerald. She assumes he is cheering on his mangy patrol. One of the vicious packs is so close she can hear saliva gurgle. Fitzgerald's shouting is closer: "Stop. Wait!" *The dogs must be out of control,* she thinks. *They must have entered the supposedly "safe" section!* She desperately tries to reach a tree when the ground beneath her disappears.

Gretchen can feel herself falling, and everything grows dark. She thinks her heart must have stopped, and she has died. *I must be having an out-of-body experience like the books describe. What's next? A tunnel? A messenger to lead me on my way?*

Everything is cloudy like a dream, and Gretchen sees the light from an opening far above her. She has read about the light at the end of a tunnel and figures that must be it. Gretchen can hear someone calling her name, but she cannot answer. Gretchen thinks she may be having a near-death experience. It seems like coming out of surgery and awakening from the anesthesia. She begins to be aware of her surroundings but still cannot respond.

Gretchen's vision begins to clear. Immediately, she sees a face in the light and faintly recognizes the voice calling her name. It is Fitzgerald. *Well, I've not headed for Heaven the way I'd hoped, but I don't want him for an escort to Hades. Can't they send the Boston Strangler or someone who will at least be sociable,* she thinks.

"Ms. Crandall. Ms. Crandall, are you alright? I tried to warn you. I've been yelling for you to stop, but you wouldn't."

"I thought you were calling the dogs. Where am I? It's chilly and damp."

"I can't hear you. You'll have to shout. But don't try to get up just yet. I think you hit your head when you fell."

"WHERE AM I?"

"You're in an animal pit. I've been having trouble with some bears fighting my dogs, so I had several of these pits dug to relocate the bears. I don't want to shoot them, and I can't let them keep hurting the dogs."

"GEE, YOU'RE ALL HEART."

"Now, now. Gently feel your head for any wounds or bleeding. Don't get up but see if anything is broken or damaged."

"MY PRIDE, FOR SURE."

"Anything important?"

"I'M HAVING TROUBLE MOVING MY RIGHT LEG, AND THERE IS A WET PATCH ON THE BACK OF MY HEAD."

"I'm going to get a ladder and flashlight. I'll be right back."

Gretchen hurts. Her back hurts, her head hurts, her leg hurts, even her elbow hurts. She cannot believe this fall happened. Looking around, all she sees is dirt and some tree roots.

Listening to Fitzgerald's footsteps recede, Gretchen contemplates what went wrong. She remembers her feelings of accomplishment at the cabana; it's hard for her to believe that things have become such a mess and even harder to accept.

With Fitzgerald gone, she rehashes her perceived stupidity. Gretchen blames herself, but she is not about to let him reproach her.

I didn't have all the facts, she thinks. *Several crucial elements were missing. I didn't know about the helicopter or consider splicing the phone wires back together. My mistake. But how could I have known about the bear pits or that Fitzgerald is an insensitive, dogmatic, self-centered, presumptuous prig! Had I known the latter, I wouldn't be here at all.*

After mentally expelling her venom, she feels the cool, loose earth in her hand from the dirt floor and remembers planting flowers with her Gramma. That was a wonderful time for Gretchen. She picks up a large clump of soil and firmly squeezes it through her fingers, letting its energy slip into her soul. She takes another handful of earth to draw more exhilaration. As she again presses the moist matter through her fingertips, something wiggles frantically for freedom. This creature immediately breaks her melodramatic state and sends her into a frenzy.

"I hate things that creep," she yells. "Especially spiders, but this was a fish worm. I hope. They aren't too bad."

Convincing herself that only harmless worms would live as deep as the pit, she has fond thoughts of Fitzgerald's return and fears for her sanity. At this point, thinking of her grandmother, she decides to stop the nonsense and make the best of the situation.

There is one thing for which she is extremely grateful. She is the only one who knows she momentarily thought she had died. In addition, this has allowed her to see another side of Fitzgerald. There is some compassion there, after all, at least for bears.

Gretchen begins to hear the rustle of the grass and the rubbing swish of Fitzgerald's jeans drawing closer. She hates to admit it, but she is relieved.

"Are you conscious?"

"YES."

"I'm lowering a box of first aid supplies. There's a flashlight on top. If you can reach it, see if there's blood on your hand from your head or if it's just wet from rainwater. After we determine the extent of your injuries and perform preliminary first aid, I'll helicopter you to the hospital. That's the fastest way."

"HOW DO YOU PLAN ON GETTING ME OUT OF HERE?"

"Oh, that shouldn't be a problem. I have a harness and a stretcher in the chopper, and I'll just use the ladder to reach you. We should be fine. Can you reach the flashlight?"

"I JUST GOT IT. UH, OH. IT'S BLOOD!"

"Don't move. I'll be right down."

"IT'S STRANGE HOW THE SIGHT OF BLOOD, ESPECIALLY YOUR OWN, CAUSES EXTREME PAIN AND PANIC WHERE LESS EXISTED BEFORE. I WONDER IF THAT'S AN INNATE REACTION OR YEARS OF

CONDITIONING FROM WATCHING CRIME SHOWS AND HORROR FLICKS."

Gretchen hears clanking and assumes it is the ladder. Then there is a sudden furor of barking dogs but no sound from Fitzgerald. She has visions of him getting eaten by a bear, which is one exclusive she does not want.

"MR. FITZGERALD, WHY ARE THE DOGS BARKING? WHAT'S GOING ON? WHAT'S HAPPENING? IS IT A BEAR?"

"No, two of the dogs are just chasing a raccoon. *Art, Jake, come. Come, boys!*"

These are well-trained dogs, and they immediately run full force to Fitzgerald as instructed. It just so happens that he is standing at the edge of the pit. When the dogs reach him, he is thrown totally off balance. Fitzgerald plunges the twenty-five feet into the hole in utter astonishment.

Chapter Seven

Ooopsies!

Aside from one rock, Gretchen was fortunate enough to land on soft earth. On the other hand, Fitzgerald came tumbling in and hit the large metal first aid box. He has the wind knocked out of him, and it takes a few minutes for the moaning and groaning to begin.

"Oh, Mr. Fitzgerald. Are you alright?"

"Please get that flashlight out of my face. I'm in pain."

"I can see that with the light."

"Please spare me your attempt at witticisms."

"Did you lose your sense of humor, or did you just never have one?"

"Look, we'll get nowhere exchanging barbs and insults. We need our energy to get out of here."

"You're right. I'm sorry. Now what? How badly are you hurt?"

"I'm not sure. I think I broke a few ribs, maybe a couple of fingers. Can you shine the light this way?"

"Sure. Ooh. Your hand looks pretty swollen already. How about your legs?"

"They feel okay."

"Can you move them?"

"Yeah, they're fine."

"Well, will you move them, please? You're killing my foot."

Fitzgerald moves both legs as well as he can in the close quarters.

"I'm sorry. Is that better?"

"Much. Thank you."

"There's not a lot of room to work, but I'm going to try to open this box. You wouldn't happen to have a screwdriver, would you?"

"No, but I have a church key in my purse."

"Thanks, but I don't think a key to the church will help."

"Not the key to the church. Haven't you ever heard of a *church-key* before?"

"Not since I was an altar boy."

"It's one of those old-fashioned can openers. You know, pointed on one end with the round..." Gretchen pauses. "You were an altar boy?" She knows this is not a good time for such a question, so she forces herself to continue. "...the round bottle cap opener on the other. Like everyone used before they invented pop tops."

"Oh, yeah. Why do you have one of those in your purse? Let me guess; pop-tops break your nails."

This man is starting to get on Gretchen's nerves. She is beginning to feel he is a sarcastic, chauvinistic imbecile. He is the person she previously respected and admired so much. She has given up her vacation and life savings to meet him.

Taking a deep breath, she squelches her urge to scratch his face, demonstrating the strength of her unbitten nails.

"Very funny. Church-keys make good self-defense weapons and take up very little room in your purse. But I have it because I get sick of getting sodas from the hotel machines. I pick up a couple of cans of juice for my room. Pineapple, tomato, grapefruit. They're tasty with ice."

"Oh, no. Don't tell me; you're a health nut."

"No. I just happen to like juice. Do you mind? Besides, you can't always find caffeine-free drinks in the machines."

"See, I knew it. You are a health nut."

"Avoiding caffeine doesn't make you a 'health nut.' That's just good common sense. It kills your B vitamins and gives you gray hair. Don't you watch the news, or can't you get it in this isolated area?"

"We're at it again. Truce?" Fitzgerald partially grins for the first time. "Let's try your church key."

It infuriates Gretchen that Fitzgerald has been the peacemaker twice, but she buries her petty anger.

"Okay. I think I can get it. My purse is right here."

After much contorting and struggling, Fitzgerald assesses their wounds. He bandages Gretchen's head to stop the bleeding. Then he wraps his cracked ribs and broken fingers to lessen the pain. Fortunately, her leg is just twisted and not damaged. Inwardly, Gretchen has to admit she is impressed by Fitzgerald's manner and thoughtful actions while attending to her wounds. This is particularly evident when he helps her sit up and lean against the dirt wall.

"Ms. Crandall, allow me. I'll support the back of your neck with my right forearm, and you grab hold of my left arm. Go very slowly. You may not want to sit up after you try this."

"Thank you. Be careful not to hit your fingers," Gretchen says.

Slowly, they start moving her upward.

"Ooooooooouuuch!" Chad winces.

"Oh no. Your fingers."

"It's not my fingers; it's my ribs. It's alright, though; just give me a minute."

It is a struggle, but Gretchen finally makes it to a sitting position. She is slightly dizzy and has the beginning of a terrible headache, but she feels better being upright.

They returned everything to the first aid box. There Chad and Gretchen sit in the rectangle hulled-hole with aggravation outweighing the pain, trying to be pleasant and avoiding accusations of blame. They stare at each other, face to face, across the flashlight on the ground between them.

Chad searches for something to say. "So, how long have you been with *The NoVa News*? And what exactly is Northern Virginia?"

"Oh, Northern Virginia, or NoVa as it's called, is the counties of Arlington, Fairfax, Loudoun, Stafford, and Prince William. And the independent cities of Alexandria, Falls Church, Fairfax, Manassas, and Manassas Park. A very wealthy area. It's a bedroom community of Washington, D.C. So, people can have a horrible commute to D.C., but their families can live a wonderful suburban life. Maryland has some traffic too, but not nearly as bad as NoVa."

"Hmmm," Chad says.

"And I've been working for *The NoVa News* since I was nineteen. A long time. I started out part-time when I was going to college. Lloyd, our editor-in-chief, promotes cherishing truth. At first, I thought he was going a bit overboard on the cherishing truth concern. But the more I listen to him, the more I really get it. Truth is all-important and should be cherished. Lloyd says being truthful is like the old saying about being pregnant; you either are or you aren't. He says that good reporters have impeccable integrity and honesty. They never skew, manipulate, or alter facts. And those who do should not even be called reporters, although a lot of them are. Lloyd says if a reporter does that, he or she has stepped into the role of being a shill for the rich and powerful and are only thinking of themselves—not the good of the people or the good of the country. He says the rich and powerful often try to buy people's souls to get them to do their bidding. They use bribery, intimidation, coercion, and, of course, money and position."

"That's interesting. Do they ever use blackmail?" Chad responds.

Gretchen freezes. Her blood runs cold, and her guilt begins multiplying rapidly. She can hardly breathe.

Finally, Fitzgerald breaks the silence. "I have a great deal of respect for 'good' reporters, as Lloyd calls them. We need more of the good ones and less of the shills." Then he kindly changes the subject. "So, how do you feel? That was a bad fall."

Gretchen is extremely relieved and thankful for the new topic. "Oh well, Mr. Fitzgerald, I am feeling much better. Sitting up helped."

"Please, call me Chad."

"Okay. I'm Gretchen. You did a great job with all these injuries. Where did you learn so much about first aid?"

"I was a medic in the Army. We often had to determine the damage without the benefit of our equipment. I'm sure at examination they'll find a slight concussion. Nothing more. We managed to correctly diagnose over ninety percent of the injuries in the field."

"That's incredible. You must have learned a lot," Gretchen pauses. "I never pictured you in any unfavorable situations, like a battle. How long did you serve?"

Chad scowls. "Hey, what is this? Always on the job, eh? You caught me off guard. I almost forgot what a conniving sneak you are. It's your unethical practices that landed us here."

Gretchen is shocked. She can't think of what to say, and when she finally gets her thoughts together, she can't get the words to come out of her mouth. *Ugh, not now! Come on, girl, think Gramma,* she tells herself. Gretchen takes a deep breath.

"Me? 'Landed us here?' Right! I dug this pit, and I am so sub-human, so uncaring that I wouldn't even let you in the house and caused you to get chased by dogs and nearly die of fright in the process."

"If you hadn't forced your way here—uninvited, trespassing—none of this would have happened," he says.

"'Uninvited?' That implies that an invitation is possible, and it isn't. I tried everything to see you, and no matter what, I couldn't get in. You're so soured on the world and so afraid of people and relationships that this hermit existence you've created left me no choice. You call it unethical; I consider it clever and innovative."

Gretchen could not believe it. She loves to feel the words flow, especially in the moment, instead of haunting her for days after an opportunity has vanished. Chad looks at her sternly. Some of what she said was true and landed with a sting.

"You say you had no choice. You could have respected my privacy and desire to be left alone. That's a choice. Then, after getting us in this mess, you have the unmitigated gall to start with the questions—your interview always foremost in your mind."

Gretchen again struggles to respond but starts faster than before. Once more, she takes a deep breath and pretends to be her grandmother.

"You think you're so smart, so intuitive. Yes, I asked questions out of interest and conversation. Interviewing was the last thing on my mind. But you haven't had social contact in so long, you can't discern the difference between prying and simple query." The Gramma approach is working, every bit as much as Dumbo's feather.

"I didn't expect you to admit it. You've got yourself a real exclusive now, eh?" Chad says with a smirk.

Pondering Chad's sarcastic question, she again thinks of her grandmother and looks Chad straight in the eye.

"Yes, if I were still interested in doing an article on you. What started this whole thing is the admiration I *had* for you. But now I think you're just a selfish, egocentric, spoiled brat! Being a millionaire and being famous makes you just that and nothing more. It doesn't make you a worthwhile person—a kind, considerate human being.

"You're nothing more than a famous, rich person. And what will you be when you're dead? What will your station in the afterlife be? Fame and wealth do not accompany you to the grave. You will just have been a statistic on some entertainment show—what a waste.

"You used to be generous and helpful. You made magic in peoples' lives. Everywhere you traveled, you would start a rec-center, build a playground, furnish someone's house, buy a family a car or home, or send some kid to college. But for years now, that's stopped. Was it all just publicity? Just PR garbage? Now you're just a soured, old recluse!"

Those words do not just sting—they deliver massive blows. The pain of these past years starts bubbling throughout Chad. The pain he has ignored, and he refused to face or even acknowledge. His jaw clenches as he suppresses the anger and devastation he carries deep inside.

"And do you know why I've become a recluse? It's because of people like you—reporters. You're always sticking your nose into my life and asking stupid questions like which side of the bed I sleep on or which hand I hold my toothbrush in. I'm sick of it."

Gretchen and Chad rant and rave for some time until they both are tired. Not from presenting their opposing viewpoints but from the lack of oxygen in that confined space with the agitated activity.

This time, however, Gretchen is determined to be the one to make the magnanimous gesture. She feels she owes it to Margaret Thatcher, Eleanor Roosevelt, and Golda Meir.

"Chad, maybe we should put our truce in writing and outline consequences of not adhering to the agreement."

Fitzgerald laughs for the first time, and something strange happens. Gretchen feels sorry for him. It seems ludicrous considering their life situations, but she sees the pain deep within his eyes she has not noticed before now. She has been too preoccupied with the grandeur of the surroundings and her preconceived ideas. However, now his pain is unmistakable.

Chapter Eight

WOUNDS RUN DEEP

Gretchen studies the sorrow in Chad's eyes. For the first time, she sees him as a person. He has always been bigger than life to her, a legend in his own time. She regrets the harsh, cruel words that so eagerly flew from her mouth like poison darts. Her grandmother was quick but never cruel.

"I didn't mean those things I said. I was just angry and defensive. I'm sorry," Gretchen says.

"Which things didn't you mean? The part about me being generous and making magic? Or the soured, old recluse?" Chad grins.

Gretchen smiles and smacks him gently on the shoulder. "You know exactly what I mean. How long before the sheriff comes?" she asks. "I heard they're pretty prompt."

"They are. But I never got the chance to call. It looks like we're going to be here quite a while," Chad admits. Trying to keep the conversation light and generic he says, "Hey, did you know that only black bears live in Georgia?"

"No. I didn't," Gretchen replies.

"They are the friendliest of all the bears. Polar bears are the most vicious, and grizzly bears come in second. Actually, Georgia is a tremendous conservation success story regarding black bears. They've done a great job. And to be clear, the black bears aren't the aggressors. It's the dogs. But a bear can kill a dog with one good whack."

Gretchen and Chad spend the next several hours making carefully guarded small talk. She does not want to offend him, and he does not want to give her material for publication. Then, quite unexpectedly, the ice is broken.

"Chad, I hate to say this. I've been avoiding it for the last half-hour, but I can't wait another minute."

"What is it?" Chad asks apprehensively.

"I've got to pee. I tried to think of a delicate way to put it, but the truth is I'm about to burst," Gretchen says, embarrassed and curling her lip.

Chad laughs. He cannot stop. "That is not at all what I expected," he says, still cackling.

Gretchen giggles nervously. "Well, females urinate too. It's just not as convenient for us. How am I going to do this?"

"Hmmm, let's see." Chad thinks for a moment and looks through the first aid box. He pulls out a collapsible cup and a knife.

"Here. You can use this," Chad says, handing Gretchen the cup. "I'll dig a hole to pour it in. It'll drain into the ground."

"This is so embarrassing. I can't believe it," Gretchen says.

"It's natural. We'll be using this hole again before we get out of here," Chad says as he digs.

Gretchen looks at the cup. "I wish it were bigger. The way I feel, I could easily fill it a good ten times."

"Be my guest. The hole's almost ready." Chad moves. "I'll stay over here with my head turned and eyes closed."

Gretchen has never been more uncomfortable in her life. However, she knows she cannot wait any longer. She has tissues from her purse and is thankful her skirt is not tight.

"I can't do this," she says. "It's too quiet. Make some noise, will you? Sing something."

Chad breaks into a deep baritone version of "Row, Row, Row Your Boat." Gretchen joins him. She is grateful that he keeps singing each time she hands him the cup to empty. Seven rounds and several filled cups later, she is finished.

"Done at last," she says, sitting in her old spot.

"Good. I thought I was going to have to dig another hole."

"That's the most embarrassing moment of my life."

Chad rubs the top of Gretchen's head. "Ah, it's okay. It's just one of those things."

Gretchen is surprised at the friendly gesture. She shakes her head. "Yeah, I've been in terrible situations before. The worst one was finding my ex-husband…" Gretchen pauses.

"You were married?" Chad asks.

Gretchen sighs. "Yes. I worked in the accounting office at George Washington University for years to put my husband through school there. It was one of the employee benefits. Looking back, I think that may have been why he wanted to marry me. Then, wouldn't you know, he leaves me for a real bimbo with an enormous chest *after* he gets his degree! She was such an airhead it was embarrassing.

"I came home early from work and found them packing his things. She even had the nerve to go through my stuff and take whatever she wanted, including my anniversary jewelry. What a loser! You think you know somebody only to find out the person you loved was just a figment of your imagination. It makes me sick to think I was so stupid."

"Don't be so hard on yourself. You couldn't know how dreadful your ex was. It's horrible you were treated like that," Chad says.

"I did get some satisfaction. Two years after they were married, the bimbo left him for a pro football player," Gretchen chuckled. "That's awful, isn't it?"

"Not at all," Chad grins.

They exchange stories of childhood disappointments, teenage adventures, and lost dreams for the next several hours. They talk; they laugh; they share crackers from the first aid box.

Chad smiles as Gretchen talks.

"...Remember, I was only six, and where we were visiting had some awesome old stuff. So, Randy and I got the rim off this old rain barrel to hold the fire. We took it into the stone tool shed and filled it with leaves. Then we tried to light a fire, but the leaves were wet, so we just got lots of smoke. That was fine with us. We started our rain dance around and around the smoldering foliage. We were just sure we could make it rain.

"The next thing we knew, smoke was billowing out of every crevice and opening of that tool shed. Here comes old Miss Williams with her broom. She probably rode it there. Miss Williams pretty much looked like Norman Bates' mother, you know, the corpse. She chased us with that broom back to the house where we were staying. I can still see her with that straw above her head and smoke rising through the air. She was screaming, 'Tiffany, you get back here!'" Gretchen laughs, and Chad shakes his head, grinning with painted memories.

Chad pauses. "Wait. Who's Tiffany?"

Gretchen stops laughing and pauses. "Ooops," she says and looks at Chad. She takes a deep breath. "Well, nobody knows it, but that's my birth name. It never fit me. It seems like Tiffanys are always pretty, and prissy, and shallow. Besides, nobody ever takes someone named Tiffany seriously. So, I changed it when I turned nineteen. I wanted something that sounded strong."

"I take it you knew a Tiffany growing up," Chad says.

"Oh, yeah," Gretchen reluctantly replies. "Our neighbor's perfect daughter. As far back as I can remember, my mother used to say, 'Why don't you wear your hair like Tiffany's?' or 'Why don't you dress like Tiffany? She always looks so cute.' Well, maybe that's because her mother did her hair and bought her cute outfits!"

Gretchen did not like remembering times with her mother. She had enjoyed all the fun stories she and Chad had shared, especially the ones about his childhood. However, this subject made her uncomfortable.

"What time is it?" Gretchen asks.

"Almost three a.m. I guess we should get some sleep," Chad says. "We've already used up one set of flashlight batteries."

Chad takes bandaging material from the box and makes a small pillow for Gretchen. "Here, use this for your head. It'll be close, but I think we'll be able to lie down and sleep."

Gretchen hates to admit, even to herself, that she is genuinely enjoying Chad's company. It has been a long time since she has spent an evening with a man, way too long.

Gretchen places her head on the material. Earlier she was so defensive; now, she finds it hard to believe how at ease she feels.

"Are you comfortable?" Chad asks as he maneuvers into a lying position, resting his legs against the dirt wall.

"Yes, thank you."

It has also been a long time since Chad has spent an evening with anyone. The words of Vance and Gretchen echo in his mind. He finds it hard to sleep. His thoughts are torturous. Maybe they have some valid points. Is it time to make some changes?

The moonlight offers a soft, warm glow to the pit. Although Gretchen is exhausted, she also finds she cannot sleep. Her mind keeps contemplating. How did all this happen? Which lucky trinket helped the most? Are miracles real? A few raindrops fall.

"There's a sheet of plastic in the box," Chad says, reaching over Gretchen and retrieving it.

As he returns to his original position, Chad is face-to-face with Gretchen, only inches apart. Gretchen does not speak. She looks at Chad. As he gazes into her big brown eyes, time seems to stand still.

Gretchen cannot breathe. All of a sudden, she comprehends how much she wants a relationship. Not with just any man, but one Gretchen loves and who loves her. She also knows she has a history of her romantic side obliterating her common sense. Too often, she has given guys attributes that do not exist and thought her Prince Charming—her soul-mate—had finally come. When, in fact, it was just another male jerk passing her way. She has learned a lot in a hard and painful way. Lessons she never wanted but that have made her wiser. Yet, perhaps she is also too afraid and far too cautious.

Chad spreads the sheet of plastic open, and it knocks Gretchen's long, silky brown hair onto her face. "Oh, sorry," he says as he strokes the hair away from her eye and cheek. He pauses and looks at Gretchen. She has a beautiful smile and is prettier than she realizes. Gretchen does not move. Chad clears his throat. "Hopefully, this should keep us somewhat dry. I'm angling the plastic to catch the rainwater in the first aid box lid. We'll need it; there's only one bottle of water left. In the morning, I'll try carving some steps in the dirt walls to try and climb out. If the dirt is compacted enough, it should work. Well, good night," he says as he lies down with his legs against the dirt wall.

"Good night," Gretchen replies as she contemplates her desires and her apprehensions.

Neither of them can readily fall asleep. They each lie in silence, hoping for slumber's sweet rescue.

Chapter Nine

ONE SCOOP OR TWO?

The early morning air is crisp and clean, floating into the pit. Fragrances mingle, bathing the senses in mellow harmony, and the sounds of nature bring peace to the marrow. Gretchen stirs.

"Good morning," Chad says softly.

Her eyes open fully. She grins and stretches a little. Gretchen is excited to see Chad's smile.

"How long have you been awake?"

"Oh, about half-an-hour. I've been watching you sleep," Chad says.

"Tell me you haven't. Did I snore? Did I drool? Don't answer that. Where's my purse? I have breath mints somewhere." Gretchen scrambles for her purse. She sees her lucky charms and gives them a gentle pat.

Chad chuckles as he watches, disregarding the pain in his ribs and fingers. Gretchen places a mint in her mouth and hands Chad one.

"Let's try this again. Good morning," Gretchen says, ignoring the pains in her head, back and shoulder. Her stomach rumbles from hunger. A sound she rarely hears. "Oh, excuse me."

"I'm sure we'll hear that a lot from both of us before we get out of here. We have a few protein bars in the first aid kit to share. We'll have to eat them sparingly so they last longer," he says as he takes one from the box and breaks it in half.

Gretchen sits up, takes her share, and bites it. "Oooooo. It's flavorful."

"Well, the fact that you're so hungry helps the taste," he says.

"Did you get any sleep?" she asks.

"I did. After a lot of thinking, that is," he admits. "Sadly, this is the most fun I've had in years. It may be time for some changes."

Gretchen's eyes widen with surprise, but she is speechless.

Abruptly, the dogs start barking ferociously and run from the edge of the pit. They can faintly hear a boat engine.

"What's that?" Gretchen asks. "I didn't think anyone was coming till Monday."

"They aren't supposed to. I don't know who that would be," Chad replies.

"Do you think they're coming here?"

"I guess we'll find out."

The noise of the boat's engine stops, and soon after, so does the ferocious barking.

"Oh, dear," Gretchen says while straightening her clothes.

Chad looks puzzled. "It has to be one of the dog trainers. They would never stop barking for anyone else unless someone's hurt them. But that can't be. We'd have heard all the dogs coming from every area of the island and absolute mayhem."

Gretchen raises her arms and tries to do something with her hair. With her arms up, her sleeves fall, revealing an awful scar on the inner part of her left upper arm. Chad gets a strange look on his face that rapidly turns to rage. He grabs Gretchen's arm.

"What's this?" he growls through gritted teeth, his anger overriding the pain in his fingers and ribs.

Gretchen is stunned. She searches for a response.

Chad is furious. "I asked you a question."

All of Gretchen's insecurities are flooding back at once. She can't get her mouth to work, something that always happened when her drunken mother would demand answers. She could not understand what was happening then or now.

"Answer me!" Chad shouts.

That phrase is all too familiar to Gretchen. She tries hard to respond and tries even harder to push the memories of her mother out of her mind. Finally, she musters a response.

"It's just a scar," Gretchen timidly replies.

Chad throws her arm back against the dirt. He turns his back to her and slams his non-injured fist into the dirt wall. The pain from his ribs causes him to wince.

"What's wrong?" she asks, touching his shoulder.

Chad shrugs her hand off and refuses to look at her or speak. His ribs and fingers ache, but his emotions hurt even more. Just as she is about to inquire again, the dogs reach the pit.

"Chad, Chad, where are you?" Sheriff Rogers calls.

"DOWN HERE," Chad yells, looking up, his fist still clenched.

The dog trainer's head appears. "Whoa. Is anything broken?" he asks.

"ALAN, JUST LOWER THE LADDER. I WANT OUT OF HERE. NOW!" Chad says to the dog trainer.

"Coming right up. Rather down, that is," Alan responds, trying not to laugh.

Gretchen tries to touch Chad in a friendly gesture. He recoils.

"What's the matter? It's a scar," she says. He ignores her.

Alan, Sheriff Rogers, and Vance start lowering the ladder into the pit. Chad grabs the feet of the ladder, places them securely in the dirt, and immediately starts to climb. The ladder doesn't reach the top of the pit, but it is close enough that Chad can lift himself to the edge of the pit.

Alan helps him stand and pats his back. "Good thing you had this ladder."

Chad nods to Alan and quickly turns to the sheriff. *"Arrest her for trespassing,"* he says, pointing to the pit but not looking Gretchen's way.

"WHAT? CHAD?" Gretchen yells.

Chad immediately storms off toward the house. Vance and the two dogs, Art and Jake, follow him.

"I tried calling you, and I couldn't find Crandall anywhere," Vance says, trying to keep up with Chad. Fitzgerald is angry and moving fast. "So, I called the sheriff's office." Chad keeps moving.

Sheriff Rogers peers curiously into the pit. "Well, you've done it now," he says.

Gretchen is in shock. She cannot believe what is happening and cannot think of anything to say, not even something her grandmother would retort. Gretchen gets her purse and slowly climbs the ladder. She is filthy. Her face and dress are covered with dirt smudges, and her dress is ripped in several places—at her right elbow, her waist, and above her right knee. It snagged on roots and rocks as she fell. When she reaches the top of the ladder, the trainer and the sheriff lift her out of the pit.

Gretchen is petrified. "The dock people kept my cell phone. I need it," she pleads.

"We'll get your stuff for you," Sheriff Rogers assures her. "But that's the least of your worries. We'll take you by the ER for treatment, and then you're going to jail."

Four hours later, Vance lectures Gretchen in her jail cell. After checking for broken bones and binding up her wounds, they cleaned her face at the ER but she is still a disheveled mess. Her back and head are killing her. Finally, she cannot take it anymore.

"Look, Senator Vance, you should believe me because I'm telling the truth. I'm not writing the story, any story," Gretchen pleads.

"Yeah, for now! You want to collect more data, more tabloid frenzy food," Vance jabs.

"I have plenty of that already. As you said, this *is* my ticket," Gretchen admits.

"So, take it and run!" he replies.

"I don't want to. I have to talk to Chad," she says.

"Oh, it's 'Chad' now. Let me tell you, if we live to be a hundred and thirty and you haven't written any story about Chad, then I'll believe you. But not until," he says adamantly.

Vance pauses and looks sternly at Gretchen. "I've cut a deal to get you out of here."

"To save your neck and avoid any publicity in your direction, no doubt," she says.

"Of course. Why else? I certainly owe you nothing but grief. Anyway, they're going to let you go. But you have to fly out tonight—never to return. All records will be wiped clean, and we will pay off all witnesses. So, whatever you do print for your story, it will be treated as fabrication," he says.

"Since I can describe the grounds so well, I know I could get corroboration. However, as I said, I'm not doing a story. I'm also not leaving. I can't. I've got to talk to Chad. Something's wrong. Something's terribly wrong."

"Chad has every right to be upset. You invaded his privacy!" he says.

"No, that's not it. We got beyond that. We shared and connected. It was beautiful. Then, just before the sheriff came, he saw the scar on my arm," Gretchen says, pushing up her sleeve. "And he went ballistic."

Vance grabs Gretchen's arm and looks intently at the scar. He glares at her with a cold, piercing stare. Angerly, he tosses Gretchen's arm to the side and stands.

"I'm out of here! Guard," he calls.

"What?" Gretchen is confused. "You're freaking out, too. Yes, it's ugly. Yes, it's a scar. But for heaven's sake, we all have flaws. What's with you?"

The deputy comes. "Ready to leave?" he asks, unlocking the cell.

"I am. She can rot here," Vance says, exiting. The deputy closes and locks the cell.

"You guys are certainly not doing much for my self-esteem," Gretchen says.

Vance sternly glares at Gretchen. "You're despicable. How dare you try to make me part of such a sick and twisted game," he says with disgust and rapidly leaves.

Gretchen stands in complete bewilderment. She is baffled and exhausted. She decides to sleep to regain some clarity. Secretly she hopes this is all a nightmare and that she will awaken to Chad's smile.

Clanging keys and jarring bars jolt Gretchen to her feet. Also, she realizes that she is in jail, and no one is getting her out. Gretchen needs to do that. As much as she hates to call Lloyd for help, she can think of no other way.

Lloyd laughs. "You're in jail? Welcome to being a real reporter! My hat's off to you. I never thought you'd do it. Well, what's the scoop? You've got the front page."

"No scoop. No story. I need you to get me out of here. Please pay whatever bail it takes," Gretchen says in desperation. "Oh, and I need Hamer to do some digging for me."

"What do you mean, 'No story?' Oh, I get it. You're going to make the most of this. I don't blame you. We're behind you all the way."

"Like always, huh, Lloyd," Gretchen says sarcastically.

Lloyd stammers. "I need an assurance from you that we will get your story or stories. I know you could go a lot of places with this, but even though we've had our differences, you've been here a long time. That should count for something."

"Oh, Lloyd, if I ever write a story, you'll get it. I promise. But there's going to be no story. It's complicated. Someday I'll explain. Right now, I just need to get out of here!"

"Of course, you've got to be scared and exhausted. Anything you say. Hamer is yours. Research, whatever. I'll transfer you to him, and I'll have you out of jail in no time."

There is silence on the phone. Gretchen hopes the call isn't lost because she is sure he meant it when the sheriff said one phone call.

"Gretchen?" Hamer's voice never sounded so good to her. "What gives?"

"Hamer, you are the best researcher and hacker I know. I need you to do some digging. Look into Chad Fitzgerald's background regarding scars. Check his childhood, his family, everything. I need clues, no matter how farfetched. Anything at all that you can find."

Chapter Ten

NOTHING IS MORE VALUABLE THAN FREEDOM

It takes Lloyd much longer to get Gretchen out of jail than expected or promised. Ultimately, he has to pull some strings with the governor's office. Sheriff Rogers is furious.

"Lady, you may have maneuvered your way out of jail. Everybody else has to wait for their bail hearing. It's not just set over the phone! But when it's time for your trial, you won't escape justice. I promise you that. We don't like shenanigans around here." The sheriff pauses. Gretchen hopes he is finished, but he is not. "And don't think you can get any info from the town folk. We've already shown your picture and warned people all over this place." He hands Gretchen her belongings and turns to the deputy. "Escort her to the door."

Gretchen remains silent. Something at which she is good but wishes she was not. Gretchen wants to ask if she can call for a taxi, although she knows she will get a hostile response. Right now, Gretchen needs fresh air and her freedom. However, she will never look at prison or prisoners in the same way. Forced confinement and constant monitoring are much worse than she had ever imagined.

Outside, she looks at the stars and breaths in the night air. Even though exhaust billows from a passing old truck, it is better than the stifling atmosphere of incarceration. Gretchen walks across the street to the gas station/convenience store to call a cab. She wants safety and a soft bed.

As she enters the store, Gretchen asks the clerk behind the counter, "Could you please tell me how far it is to the Regency Hotel?"

The clerk does not respond and waits on his next customer. Gretchen figures customers come first, so she grabs a Snickers candy bar and gets in line. When it is her turn, she asks the question again.

"Two eighty-six," the clerk responds.

Gretchen hands him a five-dollar bill and asks again. She gets only her change and no response. Then, Gretchen sees her picture taped to the cash register. She does not believe it. Gretchen turns to the person next in line and asks for directions. He looks straight through her, as if she is invisible, and gives no response. She looks around at the unfriendly faces and goes to the telephone booth, at the edge of the parking lot, to use the phone book. A phone booth is something she has not seen in a very long time.

The first listing for taxis in the yellow pages is okay with Gretchen. She bites her Snickers and calls.

"Action Taxi at your service," the guy answers.

"Please send a cab to Jack's Food & Fill-up," Gretchen says.

However, the sheriff's office had alerted the cab companies to not be readily available to any female calling for a pick up from Jack's. This is indeed a close-knit community.

"None available. It will be at least three hours."

"Never mind. Thank you," Gretchen replies and looks at the next listed number.

After calling two more cab companies and being told that none are available, Gretchen remembers what the sheriff said and realizes what she is facing. She desperately calls Phyllis.

"Help!" she cries, tears flowing.

"What's happening? Lloyd filled me in. He said you might be calling," Phyllis says with worry in her voice.

"I don't want to talk here. I'm being blackballed and need to get to my hotel. I feel like I'm back in middle school. Can you please pull up a map and tell me how to get to the Regency? I'm exhausted and a mess."

"That's scary. The map's loading. Doesn't the hotel have a shuttle?"

"Just to and from the airport."

"What about a taxi?"

"Don't ask. I need directions to my hotel fast. I'm about ready to scream."

"Go ahead. It'll help," Phyllis encourages.

"I'm afraid there might be an ordinance against it, and I don't want to end up back in jail!"

"I have the town and the Regency. What's your location?"

"The corner of Main Street and Carver."

"Oh, you're pretty close. It's only about eight blocks straight down Main. The first street you should come to is Taylor. If not, you need to walk in the other direction. I can stay on the phone with you the entire way to the hotel."

"I don't have enough battery. I'll call you when I get there."

"Be careful. And hurry," Phyllis says with deep concern.

"Thanks. I have tons to tell you when I can talk."

"It must be tough right now, but remember, with every step—*you did it*! We're all so proud of you. Oh, and Kate, Jill, and even Betty said to tell you they're praying for you. I didn't even have the heart to say something sarcastic."

Gretchen smiles. "Thanks again. I'll call ya. Bye."

"Wait. What's with this box you left on my desk with the note telling me not to open it unless something happens to you?" Phyllis asked.

"Tell you later. Got to go. It's creepy out here."

"Walk fast."

Phyllis always makes Gretchen feel better, no matter what the crisis. Beginning her trek, she is grateful that she made it to Fitzgerald, as Phyllis said. However, that quickly turns to gratitude for her friends. With every step to the hotel, she thinks about each one. It warms her sad, frightened heart, and she no longer feels so alone.

Chapter Eleven

WHAT NOW?

Gretchen struggles every step of the way to her hotel. She looks awful. Her head hurts, her feet hurt, and her entire body aches. As she makes her way through the lobby, she can feel people staring at her.

She eyes the desk area without turning her head. Behind the counter, there is a bulletin board holding her picture between activity schedules on the back wall. She hurries to the elevator as quickly as she can.

She reaches her floor and grabs snacks and drinks from the machines next to the ice maker. Entering her room, Gretchen bolts and chains the door. "I made it!" she sighs, flopping onto the bed. As much as she would like to shower, she just cannot do it. Gretchen is exhausted and does not have the strength. Only giving herself a few moments to rest, she calls Phyllis so she will know she is safe. Gretchen fills Phyllis in on everything that has happened.

"I have no idea why Fitzgerald reacted so violently to my scar, but Hamer's researching it for me to see what he can find," Gretchen says, taking off her clothes. She promises to call Phyllis tomorrow and crawls under the covers wearing just her underwear and without brushing her teeth. That is something Gretchen never does. She always brushes her teeth, but the pressure of the day has her completely drained.

At first, Gretchen is too stressed to sleep, so she munches on snacks while devising a strategy. Very quickly, she falls asleep with a Cheeto hanging out of her mouth. The night quickly turns to midday. Clang, clang, crash. Gretchen wakes with a start. The cleaning people are dropping things in the hall.

Gretchen dials the phone. "Phyllis, can you please wire me some money? I'll pay you back as soon as I can. Also, would you please overnight me the memory card with the photos of Vance I left on your desk?"

"What? That's evidence. You don't want to end up back in jail, do you?" Phyllis warns.

"It will be okay. I have a plan," Gretchen reassures Phyllis.

Gretchen takes a shower and gets a quick sandwich, then scours the town looking to interview people. She hits the flower stand, the beauty shop, the pharmacy, and the grocery store. No one will talk to her. It is worse than she ever imagined, and her picture is everywhere. Gretchen keeps going. She cannot stop trying to figure out Chad's reaction all the while. What happened?

In a desperate move, Gretchen hunts down Martin and Tom at the marina. She tries to find out who Fitzgerald's cook is and where she lives. She does not have the number or name of the detective with her who contacted the cook.

"Look, lady, you better get away from us. We want nothing to do with you," Martin snarls at her.

"You've caused enough commotion around here already," Tom chimes in nastily.

"I have money coming tomorrow," Gretchen pleads.

"You couldn't pay us enough for all your trouble," Tom says emphatically.

"Now, GIT!" Martin yells.

Dejected and scared, Gretchen walks to the park and sits on a bench. She calls Vance, using *67, so her number will not register. She knows he won't answer if he knows it is her.

Ring. Ring. "Vance here," he answers.

Gretchen swallows. "I have the memory card with your photos. Don't hang up!" She doesn't hear a click, so she keeps talking rapidly. "Let's meet and get things straightened out. I will give you the memory card. Come to the Regency Hotel pool tomorrow at three p.m. and wear swim trunks," she says.

"You're going to give me the memory card? Right!" Vance says sarcastically. "And why do I have to wear swim trunks?"

"Yes. I'm just giving you the memory card. In reality, I've been protecting you for years; I knew it was a set-up. You made a mistake but certainly not the mistake the photos make it appear. And you have to get in the pool, so I'll know you're not wearing a wire. I do not want to end up back in jail ever. Especially in this town." Gretchen starts biting her lip.

There is a moment of silence before Vance responds. Finally, he says, "You've been watching too many cop shows. Or not enough. You don't need a wire to pick up a conversation nowadays. And why in the world would I want you arrested? Shot, maybe, but not arrested. That would just spread this rubbish all around. I will meet you by the pool at three tomorrow but fully clothed."

Knowing she should not mention Fitzgerald, Gretchen refrains from asking Vance to get her in to see Chad. "Okay. I'll see you tomorrow at three," Gretchen says, hanging up the phone quickly before Vance can change his mind.

Gretchen considered giving up and going home but returning to covering the mundane is just intolerable to her. Also, she cannot forget the feelings that awakened deep inside while she was close to Chad in the pit. She has been alone far too long.

Making her way back to Main Street, Gretchen notices some pleasant aspects of the town. People are smiling and laughing as they walk. Beautiful flowers and trees with birds singing and squirrels chattering are a pleasure to see. Then she gets a strange feeling. She turns around and notices two men following her. She tries to convince herself that she imagined it, but they stay right with her. Buying some take-out spaghetti, she heads back to the hotel to retire early. It is the safest thing she can think to do. Not only does she bolt and chain the door, but she also shoves a chair under to doorknob for extra protection. She knows the police would be no help, and for that matter, the two men following her may even be cops.

Chapter Twelve

HONESTY REALLY IS THE BEST POLICY

The look on Chad's face when he saw Gretchen's scar haunts her all evening. *What is it about him and scars?* Gretchen thinks and calls Hamer. "Any luck finding something about Fitzgerald and scars?"

Hamer went through a litany of things he had found, but nothing was helpful at all. "I'll keep digging," he says.

"Thanks. I do appreciate it," Gretchen says with a sigh and hangs up the phone.

Gretchen puts her carry-out spaghetti and her notebook on the bed and lies down on her stomach. She eats some bites and sketches the pit they were in together overnight. She is searching for any clues that will help her make sense of it all. Her mind replays everything that happened that night again and again. Soon, Gretchen falls asleep with her face in the Styrofoam plate of food.

Bang. Bang. On the door. "Delivery for Gretchen Crandall." Gretchen jumps up with spaghetti hanging from her face. It is morning. She wipes the noodles from her cheek and tosses them on the bed.

"Coming," she yells, moving the chair and opening the door. It is the package from Phyllis. Gretchen signs and then rips open the envelope with much relief. She takes out a $20, the smallest bill in there, and gives the courier a tip. "Thank you," she says.

"Thank you, ma'am," he replies, going down the hall.

Phyllis is such a sweetheart. She sent Gretchen two thousand dollars. Eighteen one-hundred-dollar bills wrapped in toilet paper as a disguise and ten twenty-dollar bills. Also included is the memory card sealed in plastic and a note saying, "Let me know if you need more cash. Luv ya."

Gretchen jumps around the room in sheer delight and reprieve. "Oh, I love you, Phyllis! Thank you. Thank you. Thank you."

Catching a glimpse of herself in the mirror, Gretchen starts laughing. She has spaghetti sauce on her face and in her hair, with two noodles dangling from her ear that she had not even noticed. "Oh, for a nice, long shower."

There is plenty of time because Gretchen is not meeting Vance until three o'clock. She was unsure when the package from Phyllis would arrive, so she scheduled the meeting for mid-afternoon.

Gretchen carefully lays each of the good-luck trinkets her friends had given her on the dresser. She gingerly touches each one: the arrowhead, the rabbit's foot, the Star of David, the St. Christopher's medal, the horseshoe, the cross, and the encased mustard seed. Gretchen knows she still needs all the help she can get. She gingerly forms the items into a heart. Gretchen honestly does not know if any of them are working. However, she knows for sure that they make her feel loved.

As Gretchen starts toward the bathroom to shower, she turns back to the dresser and picks up the mustard seed. She remembers when Jill gave it to her. Jill took her by both hands, looked her straight in the eyes, and said, "To get a miracle, you have to believe in miracles. They *are* real. They positively *do* happen. You only need faith the size of this tiny mustard seed!" Jill sounded like Gretchen's grandmother.

Gretchen places it back with the other trinkets. "That sounds too simple. But how? Oh, Gramma, I wish you were here. I sure could use a miracle."

The shower feels fantastic, and Gretchen stays in a very long time. It is not like at home where the hot water runs out and turns the shower cold. This is a real treat. Gretchen straightens the room and curls her hair since she has additional time. She puts all the trinkets back into her makeup bag for her purse, except the mustard seed. Gretchen adds it to her bracelet for easy access and comfort. She is terrified to meet with Vance.

After a leisurely lunch, Gretchen goes to the pool to wait for Vance as planned. The pool area is full of lush greenery and blooming plants. It is chilly, so only a few people are there, and no one is in the water. Gretchen is thankful for that. She smells all the blossoms and touches the greenery.

When no one is watching, she slips the memory card under the dirt of a beautiful, purple flower. She sits in a chair at one of the tables and waits for Vance to arrive. The minutes pass like hours. Gretchen regrets her early arrival. She starts to bite her nails but forces herself to rub the mustard seed instead. The sun feels nice on her face. Finally, she spots Vance walking toward her.

When he gets close, Gretchen stands and extends her hand. "Thank you for meeting me," she says.

Vance ignores her hand, pulls out a chair, and sits. "Let's get this over with as quickly as possible," he says with a scowl.

"Senator Vance, I'm so sorry we met under these circumstances. I know it's hard for you to believe, but I'm a nice person. If I weren't, I wouldn't have protected you all those years regarding the pictures."

"You've told me that before. I've heard it already. You don't seem all heroic now, though," Vance says with a glare.

"Look, what I did was wrong, very wrong. And there's no excuse; I was just desperate," Gretchen admits.

"I've heard that before too. Get to the point." Vance snaps.

"The point is I am very concerned about Chad. His reaction to my scar—the look on his face; it wasn't rational. It was almost crazed. You've got to help him. Something is very wrong; I'm worried about him. The look on your face was a bit insane, too. It's a scar," Gretchen breathes.

Vance stares at Gretchen. "You have the gall to fabricate a scar to dupe Chad, then question why he's upset. You're not stable."

Gretchen is confused. "Fabricate? My scar is *not* fabricated! It's real. Feel it," Gretchen demands, pulling up her sleeve.

Vance stares at the burned impression on Gretchen's arm. It is distinctly the shape of a fireplace poker and has various colors of red, blue, pink, and purple variegated throughout the surface of the scar tissue.

Vance shakes his head. "That's even worse!"

"This was done to me. And it was excruciating." Gretchen admits, with tears welling up in her eyes.

Vance looks at her sternly. "You're telling me that you just happen to have a scar identical to..." Vance stops himself. "All the war injuries I've seen. All the V.A. Hospitals I've been to, and I've never seen a scar like that."

Gretchen leans in close to Vance. "Identical scar? Identical scar to what?"

Turning his head to the side, Vance says, "You don't know, do you?"

"Know what? I am clueless. And confused," she says.

Vance is perplexed and silent. Gretchen reaches over into the planter and takes the memory card out of the dirt. She brushes it off and gives it to Vance.

"Here. In good faith. Here's your memory card. Now, will you please tell me what's going on? Please. What's with my scar?" she pleads.

Vance is shocked she gave him the memory card. "So, how many copies did you make?" he asks sarcastically.

"None. That's the only one. I promise." Gretchen replies.

Vance stares at her for a moment, then looks her directly in the eyes. "You have an identical scar in the identical place that Kathleen, Chad's wife, got while they were married."

"What? Oooohhh. No wonder he got so upset. And no wonder he thinks I'm horrible. It all makes sense finally," Gretchen says, with a real sense of relief.

They sit in silence for several moments. Gretchen finally breaks the quiet. "Thank you so much for telling me. I've been going nuts trying to figure it out. So how did she get her scar?"

"No one knows," Vance says. "Kathleen said she tripped and fell on a log in the firepit at the ski chalet. But the injury didn't quite seem to fit. Chad offered to get her plastic surgery to repair it, but Kathleen wouldn't. She said she liked it, which also seemed a little strange. We all just thought everything else was so perfect in her life that maybe she liked the novelty of it." Vance shrugs his shoulders.

"Will you please let Chad know that I had no idea about Kathleen's scar?" Gretchen asks. "I wish he would see me."

Ding, Ding, Ding. Vance's alarm goes off on his watch. "I have to get to a meeting. I will ask Chad if he'll talk to you. I think it would be good for him. He's holding in way too much stuff. But I can't make any promises. Thank you for giving me the pictures and for protecting me. I do appreciate it immeasurably. Especially for my family. They would not have deserved all the pain these photos would have caused." Vance rushes down the street and hails a taxi.

Gretchen wishes she had said something to Vance as he left, but she could not think of any words to say. She sits in stunned silence and inwardly expresses massive gratitude for how the meeting went. Gretchen likes hearing the water fountain bubble and seeing the abundant flowers peacefully surrounding her. The afternoon meeting went better than she ever hoped.

She is thankful Vance was so open and honest. That is way more than she had ever imagined. Gretchen scratches her arm and feels the mustard seed. She pauses and is still. Maybe this is a bit of a miracle. Her luck certainly is never that good.

Chapter Thirteen

BOMBSHELLS!

Back at the hotel, Gretchen struggles about staying longer. She knows she cannot afford to stay, and it will take her a long time to pay Phyllis back. However, Gretchen cannot stand the thought of leaving yet, either. She needs to see Fitzgerald again. It will bother her forever if she leaves now. Gretchen takes the rabbit's foot out of her purse and drops it in the bathroom trashcan. She feels she can eliminate it because, as the saying goes, it certainly was not lucky for the rabbit. Plus, she thinks it is a bit creepy. However, she still appreciates the thought and loves Beth for the gesture.

Gretchen calls Phyllis and fills her in on everything. Phyllis is adamant.

"Don't be ridiculous. Of course, you're staying. So, what if you owe me money? I promise I won't break your legs." Phyllis laughs. "Besides, you've got to play this whole thing out. Who would've thought you'd get this far? Plus, a jail stint. This entire experience is priceless!" She laughs again. "You do realize I'm living vicariously through you and this adventure."

Gretchen is talking to Phyllis on her cell phone. The hotel room phone starts to flash and ring.

"Who's calling?" Phyllis asks.

"I haven't a clue. I'll call you back," Gretchen replies, hanging up her cell phone.

"Hello," she answers.

"It's Vance. Something's bothering me. Can we talk?" he asks.

"Sure. When?" Gretchen replies.

"Now. I'm in the lobby. I'll be right up," Vance says. Click.

Gretchen is glad she had not undressed, which she usually would do. She only has to put on her shoes. Had Chad agreed to talk to her? Was that even possible so fast? *That would be a miracle*, she thought.

Vance knocks on the door, and Gretchen answers. Vance immediately barges into the room.

"Please. We've got to talk! I can't stop thinking about this," he admits.

Gretchen motions Vance to the two chairs and small table by the window. "Sit down. Have you talked to Fitzgerald? Would you like something to drink?" she asks.

"No, not yet, and no, thank you. I want answers. How did you get your scar?" Vance asks frantically.

Gretchen is shocked. That is not a question she was expecting, although it seems reasonable that he asked it. She is not prepared to answer.

"Ummm. Why? What difference does it make? That was a harrowing experience that I prefer not to relive. It's personal," she explains, looking at the floor and starting to chew her fingernails.

"I'm sorry to cause you any discomfort, but it is an important question. Please," Vance says.

Gretchen just stares at him and keeps chewing her nails.

"Look, I believe from your actions today that you are sincere. I'm going to trust you. I'm going to tell you something." Vance hesitates and points his finger at Gretchen, looking her directly in the eyes. "But you have to promise me that you will *not tell* a living soul what I'm about to share with you!"

Gretchen freezes, and her eyes widen. She has no idea what she is about to hear. Swallowing deeply, she says, "I promise."

"I want to know how you got a very unusual scar, and one that is identical to Kathleen's, in the exact same place! Because Kathleen did not just die; she was murdered!" he says shockingly.

Gretchen gasps. "What?"

"That's a closely guarded secret. First and foremost, the lead detective wants the killer to think he's gotten away with it, so he'll be more likely to make mistakes. Also, Chad has just been through too much. We don't want him hounded even more than he is already. We want the case solved before any info gets out. But it seems logical that you may have some pertinent information," Vance says, opening both hands toward Gretchen as a gesture for her to talk.

"Wow. I had no idea. With that bombshell, of course, I'll try to share my gruesome tale with you." She takes a deep breath. "I dated the photographer for several months, Eddy Osborne, who works at the Senate and all over the world. You know, the one that got the pictures of you. He is extremely into high society females. Eddy is obsessed with them.

"That was not me at all. I borrowed or rented outfits to go to many of our functions. I started feeling like a phony and started seeing Eddy as one as well. Plus, I spent a lot of the time feeling quite inadequate, hanging around all these people who had mostly been made perfect with lipo, plastic surgeries, and implants. Even the guys were getting butt and pec implants. Oh, and lifts—everybody got everything lifted. It was nuts. I started wanting to break it off, but I had seen Eddy do some rotten things to people to get back at them. I had enough problems trying to get a career going without adding more grief. So, I was a bit fearful, to be honest. I just stopped trying so hard to look good, hoping he'd call it quits," she pauses.

Gretchen wrings her hands and rubs her face. She grabs some tissues and then continues.

"I think Eddy could tell I wanted out. Surprisingly, he planned this romantic evening at his house. We had a terrific dinner with all the courses, romantic music, and lots of conversation. I started thinking maybe I didn't want out. Then we had wine by the fireplace. I'm sure he drugged me because, after only a few sips, I dozed off."

Gretchen becomes agitated. She stands and begins to pace, rubbing her hands again.

"The next thing I know, six inches of the red-hot fire poker was jammed against my inside upper left arm! It was excruciating; the most painful thing I've ever experienced. I screamed like crazy. I tried to get up, but I couldn't move.

And he held the poker there! All the time claiming the whole thing was an accident," Gretchen says, crying.

"That's awful," Vance exclaims. "I'm so sorry that happened to you."

"Well, worse than that, I tried to report it to the police," she admits. "But Eddy claimed it was an accident so that the law wouldn't do anything. Plus, all his connections. I felt injured again. It was horrendous. And the abuse I endured from my alcoholic mother growing up came roaring back and just sent me into a spiraling shell. The night of the burn, Eddy sprayed some numbing stuff on the area, then bandaged my arm and drove me home. I was groggy and passing out on and off the whole time. I never saw him again. It's something I don't talk about—ever."

Gretchen sobs. Vance is unsure if she does not talk about the photographer, her mother, or both. His heart aches for her. He does not know what to do, but he has the good sense to sit there in silence and let her cry.

After ten minutes of sobbing, Gretchen's eyes are extremely swollen, and her tears begin to slow. Vance gently reaches over and pats her shoulder. "A decent cry is good for all of us," he says, placing another box of tissues on the table.

Vance's kindness touches Gretchen. She manages a smile and then starts to laugh. "Well, I never saw this coming," she chuckles.

Vance smiles. "Well, we know Eddy Osbourne is a scumbag from what he tried to do to me. Thank you again for saving my family from all the embarrassment and me from possibly losing my family. I knew Eddy was opportunistic, but I never realized he was a cruel sadist. This is terrible."

"Wait!" Gretchen slaps the table. "Did Kathleen know Eddy?"

"Not to my knowledge," Vance shakes his head. "His name is nowhere in any of the police reports. I've read them all multiple times. And Chad has hired one of the best investigators in the business, and he's never mentioned him either."

"Please, tell me more about how Kathleen got her scar? Every detail," Gretchen pleads.

"The tale has always seemed a bit fishy to me," Vance recounts. "She went on a ski vacation with a few of her girlfriends and, supposedly, fell into the bonfire when she was drunk. But her inside arm is the only place she got burned. It seems to me her clothes would have caught fire, or something else would have happened. Her friends claimed they were all passed out and didn't remember anything. However, at the time, we had no reason for doubts. It wasn't until she died that the questions started flying."

"How did she die?" Gretchen asks.

"Smothered in the bathtub," Vance says with a smirk.

"What? That's a new one. I never heard of that," Gretchen replies.

"No one else has either. The detectives assume Kathleen was smothered elsewhere, probably the bed, and then put in the bathtub. Of course, she was drunk, and they tried to make it look like a drowning. But there was not one drop of water in her lungs. Chad was devastated. It was so hard," Vance sighs.

"No wonder Fitzgerald was so mad at me. And you too. I guess it did look like I created my scar to get a story. That would be despicable," she admits. "You've got to convince Chad my scar is real and not made by me."

Vance smiles. "That won't be a problem. But we are still no closer to understanding why and how you both have identical scars. There has to be an answer and a connection somehow."

Chapter Fourteen

RISE, SHINE, AND SAGAS OR DEATHS

Gretchen is sleeping soundly when the phone rings. This time it is Hamer calling.

"Hello there, friend. Time to rise and shine. I haven't slept in two days. I have important info for you, up and at 'em. Wake up, wake up, you sleepy head. Time to get up out of bed."

"I'm here. I'm up. Are you always so chipper this early?" Gretchen asks.

"When I have important info, and I'm tired to the point of delirium," Hamer chuckles. "Listen, that guy you dated, Eddy, is a real psycho. He has been stalking high society females for more than twenty years. He has been arrested multiple times in multiple states and countries. However, consistently the charges are dropped. It seems because he has incriminating photos, and he threatens to release them publicly. I'm surprised he hasn't just gotten shot or his throat slit, but they're probably afraid the photos will surface. This guy's a real sleaze. I can't believe you ever went out with him," Hamer says.

"Honestly, I can't believe it either," Gretchen admits. "But, in my defense, like most of the sleazes out there, he puts on a good front. Most creeps don't have 'slimeball' tattooed on their forehead. It's something you have to find out, usually the hard way. We were at a boring political banquet the first time we met. We slipped outside and waltzed in the parking lot for two hours. It was divine. I felt like I was flying, and I'm not a very good dancer. It was all him. He swept me off my feet, literally. Ugh! Enough of that garbage. Please keep going. What else did you find?"

"All the high society nonsense articles frequently hitting the papers helped to track this junk. That, and I'm good," Hamer laughs. "I've documented eight different high society bimbos he's had a relationship with. And there's another one, number nine, that I'm working on getting her identity. But of the eight, three have some suspicious circumstances surrounding them. One died in a drunk driving crash by hitting a tree. She was the only one in the car and was traveling on the road to nowhere.

"A second one fell over the balcony of her ninth-floor hotel room. Splat onto the pool deck. She was drunk, of course. No one saw anything. Well, it was three in the morning, and she was the only one listed in the room. And the third one, you guessed it—drunk. She fell overboard on a docked yacht, getting tangled in some ropes on the way down, strangling. Everyone on board was asleep, and nobody heard or saw anything. Probably all drunk."

"That's unreal," Gretchen says.

"Oh, it gets more unreal." Hamer continues. "All three of those accidents happened while Eddy was dating each girl. Well, two of them did. The balcony girl had dumped him that afternoon. I think the guy's a serial killer. I don't know how he's getting away with it all. He did date other girls between the corpses, and they all seem fine."

"What kind of a time frame are we talking about?" Gretchen asks.

"For the deaths, about three years. I don't see how anybody would date Eddy; he's either a murderer or a real jinx. Girls should steer clear," Hamer says emphatically.

"Well, he can initially be quite charming, and he does take impressive pictures. He can make females look way better than they actually do. Males too. People often wait months for a photo session. And the sessions cost a fortune. He calls his photos 'works of art' and prices them like that too. A session can run $100,000 or more," Gretchen says, gesturing with her hand.

"No way! I'm in the wrong business." Hamer smacks his leg. "Why is Eddy so obsessed with high society? I don't get it. Seems pretty dull to me."

"Oh. I think it's because Eddy grew up pretty poor, and his mom was the maid for different rich people. They lived in some lavish homes in the servants' quarters. He was exposed to all the high society trappings, parties, and events, but nothing was ever his," Gretchen explains. "He also peeked through the door and listened when the kids got etiquette and manners training. Plus, Eddy watched—again peeking through the door—all the dancing lessons. So, Eddy probably learned more than the kids that were actually in the class, because he wanted to be there. Then he'd go in his room and practice. And he's a remarkable dancer. Have you found any connection between Eddy and Kathleen Fitzgerald?"

"Not yet. Eddy's still a psycho if you ask me." Hamer yawns. "I'll keep digging after I get some sleep."

"Great job, Hamer. Thank you," Gretchen says.

"Oh, and good news," Hamer shouts. "Phyllis got Lloyd to agree to pay all your expenses."

"Seriously? That is terrific news! She's the best. And you too. I'll talk to you soon."

Gretchen takes a long shower and is dressing to get breakfast. The hotel phone rings. "Hello." Gretchen answers.

"Hey, Gretchen. It's me again, Hamer."

"Well, I thought you'd be sound asleep," she says.

"I thought I would be too," Hamer chuckles. "But I couldn't stop thinking. Remember I mentioned there is a ninth female I haven't identified yet? Well, she is referred to in one of the social columns as the 'Mystery Mademoiselle.' She went to Mardi Gras with Eddy two years in a row. She has, I think, also been to countless masquerade balls with Eddy. I'm judging by her height and size in the photos. And the dimensions don't fit any of the other female Eddy dates that I've found. What if she's Kathleen?"

Gretchen gasps. "Maybe! That could be the unknown connection."

"So, if it's plausible, can you find out if Kathleen went to Mardi Gras?" Hamer asks.

"What I can find out is if she was with Fitzgerald at the time of Mardi Gras. I know she's gone on ski trips with her girlfriends." Gretchen responds.

"That would be helpful. Now I can get some sleep. Let me know what you find," Hamer says.

"I will. Sweet dreams. And thanks, again."

Click, and Hamer is gone.

Gretchen is so excited to have a possible clue. "Oh, I wish I could tell Hamer about Kathleen's murder. I've got to get with Vance." Her stomach growls. "Breakfast first." She scurries around, unplugs her cell phone, and grabs her purse. She is out of the door with a bounce in her step for the first time since she arrived here.

Chapter Fifteen

Say Cheese!

To Gretchen's surprise, Vance calls her just as she finishes her eggs.

"Meet me in front of your hotel in twenty minutes," Vance says.

"I was just about to call you. What's up?" Gretchen asks.

"Just meet me. We're going to talk to Chad, and don't be late," Vance says and hangs up immediately.

Gretchen certainly did not expect this. She hurries back to her hotel room, puts on some mascara, and curls her hair. She looks at the clock and puts on a prettier blouse. Her pulse is racing the entire time. She makes it to the front of the hotel with one minute to spare and takes a deep breath. Realizing she had not brushed her teeth after eating, she pulls out a disposable toothbrush with toothpaste from her purse and begins to scrub.

Vance pulls up to the curb and rolls down the window. "Get in," he says.

Gretchen does just that while continuing to brush. She closes the door, and Vance drives off. She spits into some tissues, placing her toothbrush in the tissues as well, and puts them in her purse.

"I have stuff to tell you, but first, what's going on?" she asks.

"Thanks for coming," Vance says in a softer tone. "First and foremost, the police captain and the private detective both want pictures of your scar. They want to compare your scar to the pictures of Kathleen's scar to see if they are identical or if it's just an illusion. Without sounding any alarms, of course. I'm taking the pictures and sending them each a thumb drive. We think that will be the safest way. Also, since your scar is real, Chad and I both feel bad about how we treated you. You're still a low-life scum reporter, and we're not excusing everything you did. However, our actions were uncalled for."

"Well, thank you. That's nice to hear," Gretchen says with a smile. "And I'm sure it doesn't hurt that you need my cooperation regarding my scar and any information I may have that could be helpful."

Vance cocks his head to the right and grins at Gretchen. "Well, that too. Now, what do you have to tell me?"

Assuring Vance that Hamer knows nothing about Kathleen's murder, Gretchen fills him in on the other deaths and the Mystery Mademoiselle.

"Could she be Kathleen?" Gretchen asks. "That could be the unknown link to Eddy."

"I have no idea," Vance admits. "But I know for sure Chad never went to Mardi Gras. He doesn't like that sort of thing. It sounds a bit farfetched but let me handle this. It will be delicate because Kathleen probably lied to Chad if she was there. That will be very painful to find out. I do not want to bring it up unless we know for sure. I'll do some checking. Kathleen had some unscrupulous girlfriends. They may know something."

They reach the marina, and Vance gets his cooler from the trunk of his car. "I brought a meal. Italian. It's always nice to talk while you eat. That way, if you hit a lull in the conversation, you can just take a bite." He smiles.

After the cooler gets inspected, they take Vance's boat to Chad's. Gretchen is incredibly nervous, and her stomach is a bit upset. However, this is a different kind of nervousness than the first trip to Fitzgerald's private island. Gretchen is unsure how she will feel when she sees Chad or what she will say.

As it turns out, Vance makes things relatively easy. He does not shut up at all. Vance directs everything. He even lays out the delicious Italian spread with Chad's most delicate china, telling Chad and Gretchen what to do every step. Gretchen appreciates Vance has taken charge. They have an enjoyable meal with pleasant small talk, including intermittent laughter.

Gretchen says, "You know, it was Eddy Osborne that sparked my extreme interest in you, Chad. I knew some about you before, but he told me some awesome stories about your actions helping people. I loved it. I started researching you and following what you did. I became a huge silent fan. There are good people around. Some just procrastinate because they don't know how to help. We need to encourage good and caring actions. Not just feelings but doings. Is 'doings' a word?" Gretchen continues without waiting for a response. "That is what you are so great at, good doings—actions that matter!"

Vance claps. "Here, here." He raises his glass. "Let's toast to all the good in the world."

Chad and Gretchen raise their glasses. "Here, here." They all say and take a drink.

However, Gretchen can't help but notice that Vance is white as a ghost.

"We need to get those pictures of your arm if that's okay. Chad has some stellar equipment. And then we need to head back. I forgot I have a meeting," Vance says.

"You have a lot of meetings. We need to do the dishes before we go," Gretchen says, a bit confused.

"I can take care of all this," Chad says. "It's been a fun time. We'll have to do it again soon."

Gretchen wants to stay and help, but she is not sure that would be the right move. Vance quickly moves things along. They take the pictures and are back in the boat all too soon for Gretchen. She does not try to talk in the boat because it is too noisy. However, she starts with the questions as soon as they are in the car.

"Vance, what happened? Why did you turn white as a sheet? Did I say something wrong?"

"Well, anybody who knows Chad knows he doesn't like accolades about his good deeds.

But that wasn't it. When you said how Eddy was talking about all the decent things Chad has done, it hit me like a ton of bricks. Not many people realize that about him. The public only knows a small portion of what he's done. Kathleen complained all the time about the good Chad did. She was not as nice as Chad is. It made it seem like maybe she *had* been talking to Eddy Osborne! And that's a scary thought," Vance admits.

Chapter Sixteen

WELL, I'LL BE

Vance starts early the following day. He couriers both thumb drives of Gretchen's scar pictures. Then Vance calls Chad's private detective and hires him to get some dirt on a few of Kathleen's not-so-nice friends fast. He wants to get to the truth for Chad as quickly as possible. Also, he wants justice for Kathleen. She liked to party way more than Chad did, but why was she killed? Nothing makes sense.

Gretchen starts early as well. She calls Hamer. "Good morning. Anything new?"

"Yes, but you didn't hear this from me. I tracked some bank records, and Eddy makes a monthly payment to Littia Newman. Blackmail maybe? It turns out they dated a while back, but only for about two months. That might be worth a visit. Also, Eddy dated his current fiancée, Wendy, a couple of different times over the years. Not for very long either time. Maybe her daddy paid him off," Hamer says.

"Please text me all the info on Littia and Wendy. I think I should fly back and see if I can get in to see them. I'll need to think of something for Littia, but I can invite Wendy to lunch to congratulate her. It seems like it's worth a shot," Gretchen says as she starts to pack.

"Yeah, why not? It beats wasting away in the hotel. But I don't think you're supposed to congratulate the girl, just the guy. Make it a celebration lunch just to be on the safe side." Hamer laughs.

"Good idea. Thanks," Gretchen responds. Click, Hamer is gone. "I've got to talk to him about saying goodbye."

Gretchen lets Vance know what she is doing and plans to be back in two or three days. They promise to keep in touch.

When Gretchen gets back home, it feels good to be there. No hotel bed or couch feels as good as your own, even if there is not as much hot water for showering.

Wendy, Eddy's fiancée, agrees to meet Gretchen for a celebration lunch, since Gretchen says she is a friend of Eddy's. Gretchen also says she may be doing an article on them to surprise Eddy. Wendy knows Eddy will love that, and Wendy loves the idea of being with one of Eddy's friends. She also loves the idea of being in on the surprise. Of course, Wendy believes that Eddy and Gretchen are just work friends. She has no idea they ever dated. Gretchen thinks Eddy will be happy with that story because he will love the idea of her doing a story on them. Eddy likes his name in print, anywhere he can get it.

Wendy is timid and does not have many friends. She still lives at home with her parents, even though she has a master's degree in mathematics.

As Wendy arrives at the restaurant, Gretchen is a bit surprised. She puts out her hand, and they shake. It is the worst floppy, limp fish handshake Gretchen has ever felt. Wendy's shoulders slump forward, her head is down, and she walks completely slouched. Whatever happened to all her posture training, or did Wendy somehow not get any? She seems like the tall girl who tries to look shorter and develops bad habits. Gretchen cannot picture her with Eddy at all. Even though Wendy is rich and very high society, she is pathetic. As they talk, Gretchen finds her pleasant and sweet but not at all Eddy's type.

Gretchen and Wendy talk for hours. Gretchen stays so long because she feels sorry for Wendy, more than gathering information. However, Gretchen learns that young Eddy watched his mother dress up like the high society ladies when they were in the house alone. She would have Eddy dance with her in the ballroom. One time they got caught, and his mother was fired immediately. They were put out on the street that night. Gretchen feels bad for Eddy as that little boy. She has to remind herself that many people have awful childhood experiences, and some have horrible childhoods, herself included. However, that is no excuse to grow up and hurt others. *We each choose whether to be good or bad, kind or evil. It's a choice! Our choice,* Gretchen thinks.

Wendy has to leave to meet Eddy. Gretchen wishes her all the best and sincerely means it. She hopes somehow Wendy does not end up with Eddy or get hurt.

Just as Gretchen reaches her house, the phone rings. It's Vance calling in a panic. "You've got to come back as soon as possible." He says frantically.

"What's the matter? What happened?" she asks.

"It's much worse than I ever thought it could be. The detective got me some good blackmail info on one of the girls, so I went to talk to her. She sang like a bird. I guess she figured Kathleen's dead, so why not? Well, I thought Kathleen might have slipped away to do some partying. And told some lies or fibs, as she would say. *No. That's not it. She was having a long-time affair with Eddy! She is the Mystery Mademoiselle.* It's going to kill Chad. He loved her so much. I need you here to help me get him to join in the investigation. We've got to get him busy and keep him busy, or who knows what will happen. He deserves to know the truth." Vance takes a deep breath. "But I don't know how he's going to take it."

"Was she in love with Eddy, or was it just the excitement of a fling?" Gretchen asks.

"What difference does that make? It might matter to a female but not to us males. Either way, Chad will be broken-hearted and devastated. I need you here to help me. Please." Vance pleads.

"I'll be on the first flight out in the morning. And calm down, or you're going to have a heart attack. We'll figure this out," Gretchen says, grasping all of the trinkets in her purse.

Chapter Seventeen

Raw Betrayal

Gretchen arrives, and Vance meets her at the airport. He puts her baggage in the back seat, and they head to the marina.

"Thank you so much for picking me up. It's way easier," Gretchen says.

"Well, thank you for coming back. I really need your help. This day is going to be rough, to say the least. I picked up subs for lunch. Something simple and no clean-up. I know Chad won't want anything to eat after we talk," Vance says in a somber tone.

"That's a good idea. You're a great friend, Senator Vance. How do you think we should handle this?" Gretchen asks.

"I've thought about it all night. I think we should have a short visit while we eat our subs. Then, if you don't mind, I think you should go to the cabana and get some sun. That way, I can talk to Chad privately for a bit. I'm sure that'll be easier on him. Not that any of this is easy, but you know what I mean," he says.

"I do know what you mean. And I am happy to go to the cabana. Honestly, I'd rather not be there for the initial discussion," Gretchen admits.

Vance hesitates. "Oh, and I found out that the scars are identical! There are differing amounts of scar tissue in some areas, but the shape, pattern, and placement are the same. That's where it will help for you to talk to him—that and get him involved in the investigation. We've got to get him off his island. Hopefully, you can get him to go back with you. I'll even come if I need to, so he won't be alone in the hotel."

"I have some ideas. I hope at least one of them works," Gretchen says.

"Don't tell me. I don't want to know. I'm afraid I may let something slip. I don't want it to seem like we're conspiring. We're planning and teaming up to help Chad. Coordinating maybe but not conspiring. His trust issues are going to be a huge problem. He's going to need a lot of healing. I'm afraid for him," Vance admits. "He's dealing with a lot. Kathleen's early death and then to find out it was murder! That's a nightmare. Now I'm adding betrayal on top of that. And betrayal that went on for years. It's going to be devastating."

"We should plan to spend the night. He shouldn't be alone," Gretchen says.

"Perfect. We're staying, and Chad can't make us leave!" Vance says emphatically.

They make it to the marina and Chad's private island. To their surprise, Chad is waving to them. Vance hasn't seen Chad like this in years, which will make the upcoming conversation even harder. Vance decides to leave Gretchen's suitcase in the boat to avoid questions. He hurries Gretchen along so Chad won't reach the boat and see her luggage. Chad may not even notice it, but Vance does not want to take the chance.

"It's great to see you guys. I'm glad you made it back," Chad admits.

Vance hugs Chad. He is so happy to see Chad chipper. How will he have the courage to ruin this first sign of healing?

"So, how long did it take you to get the kitchen cleaned?" Vance asks with a grin.

"Oh. I thought that's what you guys were here to do," Chad responds.

There is total silence, and Vance is still. Gretchen smiles. Chad puts his arm around Vance.

"Just kidding. Lighten up. It's all done." Chad laughs.

"Oh, you got me," Vance chuckles. "I brought lunch, and this time I'll clean the kitchen."

Gretchen enjoys seeing Chad happy. She knows this is going to make it much harder for Vance. They all exchange some small talk as they eat their lunch. As the sub papers are crumpled for the trash, Gretchen knows that it is her cue to leave. Fortunately, there are lots of books in the cabana.

"Well, if you fellows don't mind, I think I'd like to enjoy some of this beautiful sunshine," she says, picking up her water and walking toward the cabana.

"We're fine. You relish those rays. It's gorgeous," Vance says.

When Gretchen first left, they just kept chitchatting. Vance did not know where to start, but he knew he had to get going.

"Chad, we've got to talk. Let's go in the living room," he says. Chad could hear the somber tone of his voice.

"About what? What's wrong?" he asks as they walk to the couch and sit.

"You know I love you more than a brother. I've agonized over this, and I'm doing what I would want you to do if our roles were reversed. Truth is most important—"

Chad interrupts, "What is it? Out with it, man."

"I found out some things about Kathleen that you are not going to want to hear. But they're true! I wish they weren't—"

Chad interrupts again, "Spit it out. You're killing me here."

"Kathleen had a long-term affair with a photographer, Eddy Osborne. When she was supposedly going off with her girlfriends, frequently she was with him." Chad is stunned and sits in silence. Vance knows he needs to keep going while he can. "They attended Mardi Gras multiple times together and numerous masquerade balls. She was in costume and known as the Mystery Mademoiselle, so no one would know who she was. They also had private getaways. It went on for years. We think he is the one that burned Kathleen, not the bonfire. And he is possibly even her killer."

Chad is sitting with his head in his hands. Vance cannot see his face, but he thinks he is fighting tears.

"This can't be true!" Chad says.

"It is. And there's more," Vance continues and puts his arm around Chad. "You know how much you wanted to have children, and Kathleen was always acting like she was trying to get pregnant. Well, she was on birth control all of those years. Kathleen thought a child would cramp her style. One month she forgot to take her birth control and did get pregnant. She did not know whose baby it was, and she had an abortion."

"How do you know all this? *It can't be true. It just can't!*" Chad shouted.

"I know all of it is hard to take in," Vance shakes his head. "We both knew Kathleen had a wild streak. We just didn't know how wild. I know it's hard to believe, so I brought proof. Proof I don't want you to see, but I understand you have to."

Vance reaches into his jacket pocket and pulls out an envelope. He opens it and hands Chad a stack of pictures of Kathleen and Eddy, leaving no doubt about their affair.

Chad looks at the pictures and sobs. Vance just holds him.

Chapter Eighteen

TRUTH ABOVE ALL

After hours of grieving, Vance takes a sedative from his pocket for Chad from Chad's doctor and puts him to bed. He is hoping Chad can sleep through some of the pain. Vance sits in a chair in the bedroom with Chad in case he wakes up unexpectedly.

Meanwhile, Gretchen is still at the cabana. Fortunately, it has a bathroom and large towels to use as a pillow and blanket. She can hear noise coming from the house and dares not go there. After scanning two books and several magazines, she falls asleep on one of the Cleopatra couches. Gretchen is exhausted anyway, so this is a welcome rest.

The sun has set, and Vance is very thankful that his hard part is over. He knows it is just beginning for Chad. He hopes Gretchen can help. Vance falls asleep in the chair in Chad's room.

It is hard to fathom the ugly truths and uncovered deceit disclosed today with all so quiet and peacefully tranquil. Why do people make selfish and sinful choices that destroy them and those they supposedly love? For centuries that question has been asked. Often by those who have made the wrong choices. That is *after* they have suffered some consequences of their actions.

Just as the sun rises, a horrible sound comes from where the pits are at the hill. Gretchen jumps up quickly. Chad runs out of the house with a rifle, and Vance is close behind him. Gretchen follows.

"What's happening?" Gretchen asks.

No one answers. Chad and Vance just keep running. When they reach the top of the hill and the pit where Gretchen and Chad had fallen, Gretchen sees an enormous bear trying to get out of the pit. Chad aims the rifle and pumps three shots into the bear. He lowers the gun; the bear attempts to lunge up, and Chad fires two more shots.

"Whew. Not the way you like to start the morning," Chad says.

Gretchen looks stunned and scared.

"Oh, don't worry. It's just a tranquilizer gun," Chad says, rubbing his face. "I'll call Alan, the dog trainer. He handles all the animals. They'll come to helicopter him to the sanctuary on the mainland before the bear wakes up. Most of the bears stay on the north side of the island. We only relocate those that fight with the dogs. We've just had to transfer a few males. And the males are pretty solitary creatures, so they do well in the new environment. I try to be fair. The bears were here long before I came.

"But we had to get this guy before the dogs get out, because old Bilbo would jump right in the pit with him. He thinks he could take him, but that bear would tear him apart! Bilbo has way more chutzpah than strength. Like those little Yorkshire Terriers that act all ferocious, but you could just pin them down with your thumb. But nobody ever does because they're so cute to watch. Bears don't like the smell of pine, so we use pine oil as a deterrent. But some still come to the house area anyway. I bet this guy weighs at least five hundred pounds. Did you know bears have litters of cubs just like cats have litters of kittens?"

Vance knows Chad is tired and is rambling a bit. Gretchen stands in silence. She is shocked by the bear but more stunned by how bad Chad looks. His eyes are almost swollen shut, and his whole face is puffy. Vance comes to the rescue, even though he is surprised by how well Chad is talking.

"Good shooting. This adventure is the most exciting morning I've had in a long time. Well, maybe ever." Vance laughs. "Let's go get some breakfast. I'm starving. That sub is long gone."

They all go to the house and keep the conversation light. Chad calls Alan to get the bear, then he makes bacon and pancakes. Gretchen and Vance just set the table. They want to keep Chad as busy as possible. To their surprise, Chad makes the pancakes for each of them in the shape of Mickey Mouse with lots of butter and heated, real maple syrup.

"I love Mickey Mouse," Gretchen says. "I hate to cut this."

"You won't after you take a bite," Vance says. "This is delicious. I think these are the best pancakes I've ever had. What kind of butter is this? It's scrumptious."

"It's Finlandia from grass-fed cows in Finland," Chad answered. "It's all I use anymore. I love it."

"Ummm. These are the best pancakes I've ever had, too. You're right," Gretchen gleefully says.

"Well, thank you. And the fact that they're shaped like Mickey makes them even better," Chad adds.

"What's with Mickey Mouse?" Vance asks.

"Well, Walt Disney is one of my heroes," Chad confesses.

"What? I never knew that," Vance says.

"Yeah. Walt didn't have a great childhood, and he wanted to make things better for other kids. And he did!" Chad declares.

"I think he made things better for all of us," he continued. "And I think we should all think like that too, wanting to make things better for others. And Mickey reminds me of that. Often.

"The company has its ups and downs, depending on who's in charge. But Walt and Mickey will always stay true to their mission."

"Oooh, there's a Mickey clock and a Mickey snow globe." Gretchen points to each. "I love them."

"I never noticed those before. That's pretty cool," Vance adds.

"Mickey helps remind me that there is goodness, and there are good people in the world. Sometimes you need to remember that because it's easy to forget. Especially with all the bad around," Chad says, looking sad.

Gretchen finds some important words. "That is fabulous. Mickey always helped me escape my garbage growing up. And I'm still a huge fan. My favorite nightshirt is Mickey. Vance, we've got to get you a Mickey t-shirt."

"Wait," Chad says. "I don't think I've ever even seen you in a t-shirt. The most casual he gets is a golf shirt. We're going to change that. You've been hunting bear now, so you've got to loosen up." They all laugh.

Gretchen raises her glass of orange juice. "To Mickey." They all toast, "Here, here to Mickey." The glasses clink, and they do a high five with their left hands. Gretchen's left sleeve drops, exposing her scar. Everything becomes silent.

Chad looks down slowly. "I guess we've avoided the inevitable long enough. So how did you get that scar?" he asks.

Gretchen is silently chanting, *"Help me, Gramma! Help me, Gramma. Help me, Gramma."* She takes a deep breath. "Well, I've been thinking about that a lot lately. I used to avoid thinking about it at all. And I've realized two things I didn't know before. Number one: I only took a few sips of my drugged wine before I passed out. I think the plan was that I drink all the spiked wine so that I wouldn't wake up. I wish I had because it was excruciating! And number two: It's foggy, but I remember seeing ropes. I was tied up. That's why I couldn't move." Gretchen relates the same story to Chad that she had told Vance. She found it easier to tell this time, and although she cried, it was not nearly as much as when she had told Vance. *Maybe tears do have some healing power. That or Gramma really is helping me,* she thinks.

"Thank you for telling me. I know that wasn't easy," Chad says. "May I see your scar?"

Gretchen holds out her left arm toward Chad and raises her sleeve. Chad looks closely.

"That does look like Kathleen's scar. Eerily so," he says and gingerly places her arm back down on the table.

Gretchen tells Fitzgerald about her relationship with Eddy the same way she had told Vance. However, she also includes the part about them dancing the first night the way she had told Hamer. This description helps them understand more about how charming Eddy can be. She hopes it makes her look a little better and not quite as stupid.

"This helps me a lot, Gretchen. Thank you again. You're a good friend," Chad says and changes the subject. "How about some hot chocolate for everybody?" Chad asks.

"Sounds good to me," Vance says. "Nothing like hot chocolate to warm your belly."

"And your soul," Chad adds.

Chapter Nineteen

BULLETS ANYONE?

Vance is impressed by how well Chad is handling the devastating news about Kathleen today. Last night he thought Chad might have to be hospitalized. He is sure Gretchen being there helps. They spend the day enjoying the surroundings and watching the bear get hoisted into the air, limp as a rag in his massive harness.

"You should be filming this, Chad. It looks like a cartoon," Vance says.

"I didn't know this could even happen," Gretchen admits. "It's fascinating."

"Now we just have to figure out a good trap for that murdering Eddy," Vance says.

"I like the shooting part," Gretchen says with a smile. "But with bullets this time."

"We don't want anybody but him ending up in jail. For sure. And shooting's too good for him anyway!" Vance says.

Chad was quiet. Gretchen looks at Vance and then Chad.

"Chad," she says, looking directly at him. "There's something I'm hoping you can help me with. We need to talk to a lady named Littia Newman. I can't figure out what her deal is. Like many of his involvements, she and Eddy only dated about two months. Most of them don't last very long."

"Well, yeah." Vance interrupts. "He's a creep!"

"True," Gretchen continues. "But it seems to be lasting with his current fiancée, Wendy. She's rather sad. I feel sorry for her. Hamer thinks Eddy is just holding out for a huge payoff from the dad. He's loaded." Gretchen looks at Chad. "Well, I guess you are too," She laughs.

"Not appropriate," Vance chides.

"Back to business." Gretchen smiles. "Hamer tracked monthly bank payments that Eddy has been making to Littia for four years. We wonder if she's blackmailing him with something. Will you go with me to talk to her? Hamer says she does much better with men than women."

"Sure. I'll go. We've got to put an end to all this pain," Chad remarks while deep in thought.

"What I don't get is how Eddy has gotten away with all this," Vance states.

Out of nowhere, Gretchen asks, "So why do you have three pools? I can see the one is for diving, but what about the other two?" Chad does not respond and walks toward the house.

With Vance spearheading the planning, they decide to spend the night and leave early the next day. Even though Chad seems to be doing remarkably well, Vance still does not want him to be alone. He knows how often people put on a good front and hide what they are genuinely feeling and combating deep inside.

Chapter Twenty

REFLECTING IS GOOD

Vance takes Chad and Gretchen to the airport and drops them at the front door. It has been an ordeal, but the truth is essential. Chad appreciates Vance's friendship. He and Vance hug. Then, for the first time, Vance hugs Gretchen.

"Now, you guys, be safe and keep me posted. I'll be back in D.C. in two days. Be careful. This guy's horrible!" Vance warns.

"We'll call you," Gretchen assures Vance.

Gretchen is touched by Vance's hug. She is also highly thankful the hostility is gone from both Fitzgerald and Vance. That did not feel good at all.

Gretchen had parked her car at the airport, which will work well. They will have time to eat and then meet Littia at her office. She did not want them to come to her house when Gretchen made the appointment.

The plane flies over Washington, D.C.

"Look." Gretchen points. "There's the Washington Monument. George Washington is my favorite Founding Father," she says excitedly.

Chad grins. "Oh, yeah? Why's that?"

"He's my hero. He was way ahead of his time. He died December 14, 1799." She touches Chad's arm. "He died of bloodletting, which was a painful and very gruesome death. It was a horrible practice back then that they thought would help, but it did the opposite. But he's my hero because he gave his slave butler and good friend his freedom early, and then George ultimately gave all his slaves their freedom. That was before England or any country had abolished slavery.

"Some of the Founding Fathers, including George, tried hard to abolish slavery in America from the beginning, but there were too many people in opposition to it to make it work then. George had over a hundred slaves. His wife, Martha, had more slaves than he did, some from her previous marriage that she got when her husband died before she was with George. But she also gave them all their freedom on her part.

"Way back then, George Washington did the right thing, and people don't always do that," Gretchen stops and takes a deep breath.

"Interesting. I didn't all know that," Chad says with a big smile, and Gretchen smiles back.

"Hey, do you want to grab some food and have a picnic on the Mall by the reflecting pool?" Gretchen asks.

"Sure. Sounds good," Chad answers.

A flight attendant makes an announcement over the intercom for passengers to prepare for landing. Gretchen is feeling good that things are going well with Chad so far. It is nice to be friends.

As soon as they enter Gretchen's car, she asks. "So, what's your favorite food? What do you like to eat?"

"I'm pretty easy. I eat just about anything," Chad replies.

"Yeah, with your delicious butter from Finland, I can't buy that," she says.

"It's true. And you can get that butter in lots of places in America. It's not like I have it flown from Finland. Just pick something. I'll like it," he says.

"That's a dangerous promise. Do you like sauerkraut?" Gretchen asks.

Chad chuckles. "Yes, I do."

"We don't have a huge amount of time, so I'll surprise you," she says, smiling and sending a quick text.

Gretchen drives them to the Hawk and Dove. "Wait right here," she says and hurries into the restaurant. She quickly runs out with two bags, and they go to the Washington Mall.

"I'm holding you to your statement," she says with a laugh.

Gretchen parks the car and grabs the bags and a blanket from the trunk. It is a beautiful day, and the grass is bright green. They walk to the reflecting pool, spread the blanket on the grass, and sit down for a picnic. They can see the whole Washington Monument reflected in the water.

"I hope you like this sandwich. It's one of my favorites," Gretchen says, opening the sandwiches and handing Chad one and a bottle of natural lemon-flavored water.

"I love Reubens. How did you know?" Chad asks.

"Seriously? You like them?" she asks.

"Yes. I do," Chad says and ravenously digs in.

"That's a relief. I'm sorry. I think I got a little carried away. I usually come here by myself when I need to think about things," Gretchen admits.

"When you need to do some reflecting?" Chad asks with a chuckle.

Gretchen laughs. "No, you didn't just go there? That was good." They both laugh.

"Speaking of good, this Reuben is delicious," he says emphatically.

Chad and Gretchen enjoy their picnic. It is fun bantering and is a break from the horror they will be investigating.

They arrive at Littia's office right on time. She is a CPA with a large firm. The receptionist takes them back to her very plush office.

Gretchen extends her hand as she walks to Littia. "Thank you so much for seeing us."

Littia shakes Gretchen's hand and then Chad's. Littia motions to the chairs facing her desk. "Please, have a seat," she says.

Gretchen is a bit shocked. Littia is not at all what she was expecting. She is intelligent, competent, impressive, and a CPA. Not the pretty-but-ditzy type Eddy usually dates. Plus, she is gorgeous. Gretchen was expecting Littia to be the receptionist or working for her *daddy's firm,* not holding her own because she is intelligent and capable,

"Thank you," Gretchen replies as they sit. "Have you met Eddy Osborne's fiancée, Wendy, yet?" she asks, grasping for something to say.

"No, I haven't," Littia responds.

"Well, I'm considering having a bridal shower," Gretchen says, trying to get a conversation going.

A conversation does start, but it is between Littia and Chad. Hamer was right about her liking males, and Gretchen wonders how he knew that. Littia is laser-focused on Chad, and she keeps a conversation going until nightfall. Gretchen does not interrupt because she hopes to glean something from the exchange relating to Eddy. However, after more than two hours, she only garners that Littia is interested in Chad.

Finally, Chad goes fishing for some information. "So, how well do you know Eddy?" Chad asks Littia.

"Not very," she replies and looks at the clock. "I didn't realize how late it is. I am so sorry, but I have to go," Littia says as she stands and then shakes Chad's hand for a longer than usual time. "It has been such a pleasure to meet you."

Even though Littia ignores Gretchen, Gretchen reaches over and shakes her hand.

"Thank you for meeting with us, Littia. I'll be in touch about the bridal function. Sorry, we kept you so late," she says as they walk out of the office.

Exiting the building, Gretchen comments, "Boy, when you mentioned Eddy, she couldn't get rid of us fast enough!"

"That's for sure! There's something fishy with them," Chad says.

"Yeah, and we need to figure out what it is," she responds.

Chapter Twenty-One

THE HAMER HAMMER

Gretchen drives Chad to Hamer's parents' house, where she has made arrangements for him to stay. Chad wants to go to a hotel, but Gretchen insists he stay with Hamer. Vance is still concerned about Chad being alone, and Gretchen only has a small one-bedroom apartment. It works out well. Hamer is house-sitting his parents' massive place in Virginia while they tour Europe.

Hamer is grilling shish kabobs with his dad's homemade sauce. They arrive just in time. Gretchen texted when they left, and Hamer is an excellent judge of driving times.

"Hey, guys. Come on in," Hamer says with a huge smile. He is a bit excited about having the famous Chad Fitzgerald at the house.

"Wow!" Gretchen says. "This place is beautiful!"

"My mom will be so happy you said that. Thank you," Hamer says.

"It's very nice," Chad adds.

"Mom is going to have a cow knowing *you* said that. Thank you. It's a real honor to have you here, Mr. Fitzgerald," Hamer says, putting his hands up from excitement.

"Please, call me Chad. And I'm just an ordinary guy, like everybody else."

Gretchen is starting to question if having Chad stay with Hamer is a good idea. "Well, not quite like everybody else, but close enough. He's a good guy. Now, don't I smell something delightful?" she says, trying to change the subject.

"Oh, yes. Please put your bag in here, Chad," Hamer says, motioning to the bedroom. "It's a guestroom with a full bath. And then we'll all go to the kitchen."

Chad puts his bag at the bedroom door, and they follow Hamer to the kitchen.

"The kabobs are ready, and I have them in the warmer," Hamer says.

"This looks yummy. Is it a cheesecake?" Gretchen asks.

"It's the best cheesecake on the planet. Homemade pumpkin cheesecake my mom made and put in the freezer," Hamer says, nodding his head.

They have a nice dinner, and Gretchen makes sure the conversation stays light.

"The sauce on the kabobs is excellent. The best I've ever had. What is it?" Chad asks.

"That's my dad's specialty. It's Worcestershire, wild blossom honey, and Texas Pete. I'll get the ratios for you. He loves to share his recipes," Hamer says.

"Well, this pumpkin cheesecake is the best cheesecake I've ever had," Gretchen adds.

"I told you. Let's move to the living room. I have some hot chocolate steaming that you're also going to love. A little birdie told me that hot chocolate is a favorite of everybody," Hamer says.

They all go to the living room and enjoy their hot cocoa.

Chad looks at Gretchen and then at Hamer. "Do you think Littia Newman may be just getting paid because she's Eddy's accountant? After all, she is a CPA."

Suddenly, Hamer slams his cup on the side table. "Oh, it's more likely blackmail than tax service. I have something to tell you. But neither of you can tell anybody because it was kind of illegal," Hamer says, wringing his hands.

"We will not tell a soul. We promise. But don't get yourself in trouble," Gretchen says and looks at Chad.

"Yes. Promise," Chad adds.

"Littia Newman has had reconstructive surgery on her upper left arm for scar removal! *For certain.* And it's going to take further surgeries to complete the job. Don't ask me how I know, but it is a *fact*," Hamer says and puts both of his hands on top of his head.

"What? You're serious?" Gretchen exclaims.

"Totally serious," Hamer responds.

They have a deep discussion for the next forty-five minutes. Then, Gretchen jumps up and screams.

"Wait. I've been trying to make sense of all this burning of females. Who does that to people and why? The cruelty of it. What if Eddy is branding girls as his? Like cattle. Only much worse. We don't have hide; we have skin that hurts like crazy. I read that some sex traffickers brand or tattoo their sex slave victims as proof of ownership. It's sick and disgusting!" Gretchen snarls.

"It's evil!" Chad adds emphatically.

Chapter Twenty-Two

SWISH!

Gretchen didn't leave Hamer's until almost four a.m. She tossed and turned most of the time she was trying to sleep. Her apartment was quiet, but Gretchen could not get her mind to stop thinking. She wants to see if she can find out anything about Littia from Wendy. She gets up early and calls Wendy at eight a.m., figuring Chad and Hamer need to sleep late. Wendy is excited and tells her to come on over. She meets with Wendy at her house under the ruse of discussing a bridal function.

On the way to Wendy's, Gretchen calls Vance. "Hi, it's me," she says. "Chad is okay. We've been keeping him too busy and too engaged to think. And under protest, he's staying with Hamer."

"Impressive job. Thank you," Vance says.

"Well, that's what I want to talk to you about. I'm not so sure it's a good job. I've been thinking about what my Gramma used to say. She always said, *'The only way out of pain is through the pain. If you don't get past the pain, you bury it and carry it with you for the rest of your life. Or until you face it and feel it.'* She always said that's why my mom's an alcoholic. She refuses to deal with the pain that she's had. Gramma said people think that ignoring the problem or pain doesn't bother or affect you. *'But in reality, it controls and often destroys you,'* in many ways people don't get. Everybody knows about individuals turning to alcohol or drugs or both, but she warned of many other dangers. Becoming soured, or cynical, or mean, or hateful, or vicious, or cruel, or distrustful, and the list goes on. I don't want any of that for Chad. We need to let him grieve."

"Your Gramma was one smart lady. That makes sense. I tell you what, let's get through this investigation nightmare, and then we'll make sure Chad gets time to grieve. And that he does. I promise," Vance says.

"That works. Thanks. I've got to go. Talk to you soon," Gretchen says as she parks her car and goes to Wendy's door.

Wendy is thrilled to have Gretchen at her house. She has an assortment of pastries waiting on the table. They exchange chitchat, and Gretchen directs them to get down to business. First, they make lists.

"You are so sweet to do this," Wendy says.

"So, who all should we invite?" Gretchen asks, with her notebook and pen in hand.

"I'm not sure. I'll have to think," Wendy replies.

"What about Littia Newman?" Gretchen suggests, hoping to learn something.

"Who?" Wendy questions.

"Littia Newman," Gretchen repeats.

"I don't know who that is," Wendy says, and Gretchen's heart sinks.

Gretchen spends the next hour trying to get any helpful information. Even names for Hamer to research. However, she keeps hitting dead ends, but now she feels like she may need to do some sort of bridal celebration to relieve her guilt.

Not getting anywhere with Wendy, Gretchen decides to confront Littia without Chad to see what she can learn. With her testimony and Littia's, they should be able to charge Eddy with something, unless it has been too long. Going to Littia's office, she keeps telling herself she must be careful not to break her promise to Hamer.

Gretchen buys two to-go orange juices from the carry-out next to Littia's office building. She carries them very visibly and greets the receptionist.

"Good morning. Nice to see you again. I'm going to Littia office," she says. Gretchen keeps walking right past the receptionist and down the hall to Littia's office. She is hoping the whole time that Littia is alone. She assumes the receptionist would stop her if she were with somebody.

Gretchen can see Littia is by herself through her large glass walls. She opens the door, holding both cups in one hand. Gretchen pops her head and the OJ into the room.

"We need to talk," Gretchen says. Littia initially gets angry. "About a couple of things and Chad," Gretchen continues. As soon as she says 'Chad,' Littia's face softens. Gretchen steps into the office.

"So, are you and Chad dating?" Littia asks.

"Oh, no. Not at all. Just friends," Gretchen replies and thinks, *don't I wish.*

"Have a seat," she says, motioning to the chair.

Gretchen closes the door, sits down, and hands Littia an orange juice. She spends a couple of hours trying to get Littia to open up about Eddy, but the conversation always gets back to Chad. Gretchen thinks Littia should be an attorney instead of a CPA. It is hard because Gretchen cannot mention her arm or that Littia is getting payments from Eddy. Finally, Gretchen takes a shot.

"Look, Chad's a nice guy, and I know you dated Eddy, and he's not a nice guy. I don't want Chad getting hurt. I just need to understand, what's the deal?"

Littia tries to avoid saying anything, but Gretchen is relentless. At last, Littia admits she dated Eddy for a short time and how wonderful he is. She even tells Gretchen that Eddy paid for a surgery she needed. Of course, not saying what kind of surgery. Littia says she would never say anything negative about Eddy.

Gretchen keeps pressing. She knows Littia is only talking to her because she is interested in Chad. Accidentally, Littia lets it slip that Eddy has some indiscreet photos of her. Now, Gretchen understands why she will not condemn Eddy. She is protecting herself. However, it does not explain the payments. Maybe she is blackmailing him.

Realizing it is futile to stay any longer, Gretchen leaves. She is not a liar or a deceiver by nature and feels extremely bad about manipulating Wendy. However, it is not bothering her one bit about Littia. She seems pretty savvy and shrewd. As soon as Gretchen steps out of the office, she receives multiple texts and missed calls registering. Hamer and Chad have been trying to reach her.

Oh, Littia must have one of those devices where cell phones won't work. That way, no one can record anything in her office. She is devious and smart, Gretchen thinks. Then she calls Hamer.

"Hey, what's up? My phone wasn't registering," she says.

"Are you okay? We've been worried."

"I'm fine," she says.

"Well, then, another mystery solved. We think. With Chad's help," Hamer says enthusiastically.

"What is it? I can use some good news. I've been striking out all day."

"I made a big wall chart of all the info I could find on Eddy, Littia, Kathleen, Wendy, and the dead girls to try to make sense of things. There are years of info from the high-society garbage columns. And I'm surprised how many garbage columns there are. I made a timeline, so to speak. Littia Newman has a son named Winston. She was given a huge deal baby shower that, of course, hit the high-society column. Chad realized that his birth calculates to her getting pregnant during the two months she dated Eddy. Chad figured that out. We think the payments are possibly child support. Bingo. Slam dunk. Swish. At-a-boys. We think," Hamer says.

"Whoa—That sure would answer a lot of questions. Terrific job, guys. I'm very impressed," Gretchen responds.

"Well, Chad is taking us out for a celebration dinner at some posh restaurant. Oh, and we don't think Littia's husband knows that the boy isn't his. Although, we're just guessing on that," Hamer confesses.

"What? She has a husband? She sure doesn't act like it." Gretchen is shocked, especially after the way Littia flirted so blatantly with Chad.

"Yeah, who knew? Littia and her husband split up for about six months during the time she was dating Eddy. But they got back together. Boy, their anniversary party was huge," Hamer says.

"That would sure clear up some questions if it's true about the kid. But right now, I'm dropping over. I hardly got any sleep. I'm going home to take a nap," she says, yawning.

"Go get some sleep, and we'll pick you up at eight," Hamer says.

"Deal. Sounds good," Gretchen says and hopes she can make it to her bed without falling asleep while driving.

"Hey, Gretch, we're going to nail this torturing, murdering, evil psycho yet!"

Chapter Twenty-Three

FIT TO BE TIED

Gretchen makes it to her bed, sets her clock to get ready for dinner, and immediately falls deep asleep in her clothes. Hamer's last words were very reassuring. She treasures his friendship. She is very grateful for Chad's, as well. For some reason, Chad helps her feel more confident. She is pleased with how she handled Littia. Maybe it is because Chad is a truly good person and reminds her of her Gramma.

Bam—Bam—Bam! On the door. Gretchen is sound asleep but awakens with a start. *Did I not hear the alarm?* She wonders. She stumbles out of bed and down the hall to the door. She looks through the peephole, but it is covered—something Hamer would do. She opens the door.

"Sorry, guys. I was—" Before she can finish her sentence, Gretchen is knocked to the ground by a hit to the face with a large hand. The door slams shut. Eddy is standing over her, and he is furious.

"I thought you would know not to mess with me. Or anybody that belongs to me. Littia is off-limits. Wendy is off-limits. And you are not doing any bridal nonsense, 'cause you won't be around."

Gretchen never thought her prying would get back to Eddy so soon, especially since she told Wendy she wanted to surprise Eddy. She assumed he would be in jail before he was a danger to her. His threat of her not being around, coupled with her knowledge of the murders, horrifies Gretchen. At this point, she fears for her life! All of her insecurity rushes back at once. *Gramma, please help me,* she pleads in her mind. She looks at the clock. It is seven-forty. Gretchen realizes that Hamer and Chad will be here in twenty minutes, and the door is unlocked. Eddy just slammed it. He grabs her by the hair.

"Look, Eddy, if you don't want me to do a bridal shower, consider it canceled. I was just going to have Littia help with the shower. She sure thinks you're a great guy." Eddy picks Gretchen up with one hand by the throat. "How do you even know about Littia?" he growls.

"A long time ago, I saw a picture of you two together on the society page when you were dating. She's quite a catch."

"Yeah, she's been good to have. The best," Eddy says.

Gretchen now knows that Littia's son *is* Eddy's. She must keep stalling.

"And Wendy, she's at the top of the socialite ladder. You've done well for yourself. You hit the jackpot with her. You've got to feel great about that," she says, trying not to vomit.

Eddy throws Gretchen onto the couch. "Respect. I've gotten lots of respect with Wendy," he says.

"I remember when we danced in the parking lot that first night. It was magical. You are quite the catch yourself. How do you do it? How do you get all the girls?" she asks.

Gretchen's eye was hit hard with Eddy's hand. She can feel it swelling a lot, and her voice starts to crack from being choked.

"Charm, I guess. That's what I hear the most. 'Oh, you're so charming,'" he says,

"Well, if you don't want me to come to the wedding, I won't. But I sure would love to watch you dance. You're the best dancer I've ever seen. How did you get to be so good?" she asks.

Gretchen hit the jackpot herself with that question. Eddy starts telling the tale of his childhood, and how he had taught himself to dance by peeking through the crack of the door while the lessons were taught. He had learned every dance style and was much better than all the kids in the classes. She got him to describe and demonstrate every dance step in intricate detail.

At last, there is a knock at the door.

"Who's that?" Eddy snaps.

"Come in," Gretchen yells with her raspy voice. *"Help!"*

Hamer opens the door with Chad right behind him; they see Eddy and the condition of Gretchen. Eddy lunges at Hamer. Eddy is way bigger and rougher than both of her rescuers. Surprisingly, Hamer is a black belt in karate and starts using his training. However, he has never been in a real fight. He has only beaten opponents in matches where everyone follows the rules and politely bows when finished. It is not going well. Chad promptly picks up a metal lamp and smashes Eddy over the head as hard as he can. Eddy hits the floor hard.

Gretchen starts crying, and they both run to her.

"Are you okay? How bad are you hurt?" Hamer asks.

"Do you need an ambulance?" Chad asks at the same time.

"I'm okay. I'm so glad you guys made it in time. I thought I was a goner! Thank you," she says, with tears flowing.

Eddy starts to stir. Hamer walks over and hits him with the lamp again.

"We need to call the police," Chad declares, taking his phone from his pocket.

"No," Hamer responds and grabs Chad's hand to stop him. He closes the door. "This is Gretchen's story. She needs an exclusive. If we call the police, this place will be crawling with news crews and reporters."

Chad looks at Gretchen. "He's right," she says. "An exclusive would be nice. My first one."

"You've certainly earned this one," Chad says, with caring in his voice and eyes.

"I've got zip ties in my trunk. We'll subdue Eddy and take him to the station. I know the captain and the head sheriff at the Maryland State police. They're great. We want them handling this. The county law is good, but they're better. Don't touch anything. Don't change your clothes or wash up. Just get your story written. They'll be taking pictures and fingerprints. But it wouldn't hurt for us to get some pics, too. Please take some pictures of Gretchen while I get the zip ties," Hamer says to Chad and goes to his car.

"I'm so sorry this happened to you," Chad says, sweetly smiling at Gretchen. "Your beautiful face is swollen and bruised and still swelling more. You need some ice, but Hamer's right, and you shouldn't do anything yet. But I have to say, this is a bit extreme to get an exclusive."

They both laugh. Chad focuses his cell phone on Gretchen's face.

"Say *exclusive*," he says and takes photos from different angles.

Hamer returns and binds Eddy's feet and hands behind his back with the zip ties. Then Hamer and Chad struggle to get Eddy to the car. Eddy is tall and muscular, but they manage to put him in the back seat.

"We need to have his hands behind his back for safety. If they're in front, it's way too easy to get someone in a choke-hold. Many prisoners have escaped that way," Hamer says. "Do you think he's okay? I didn't kill him with that lamp, did I?" he asks.

"He'll be fine. A headache, maybe, but scum is hard to destroy," Chad reassures Hamer. "Those sure were some excellent kicks you did in there. I know a few moves but nothing like what you were doing," Chad says, trying to make Hamer feel better. It works, and Hamer smiles.

They get Eddy sitting upright and fasten his seatbelt. Then Hamer does something Chad would never have thought of doing. He connects zip ties and wraps them around Eddy multiple times and around the seatbelt, pulling them securely.

Chad smiles. "This guy's not going anywhere."

They head to the police station with everything secure so that Gretchen will be guaranteed an exclusive.

Chapter Twenty-Four

REALLY?

Gretchen works as quickly as possible to complete and review her article. She cannot believe this is happening. It is such a leap from the basket-weaving type material she has been stuck reporting for a long time. Appreciation fills her heart for not only this opportunity but for Hamer, Chad, and shockingly, Vance and even Lloyd.

She does one more read-through and decides it is ready to submit. She hits send. As she closes her laptop, there is a knock at the door. Gretchen assumes it is Hamer and Chad or the police. However, she will not open the door until she can see who it is. A lesson she will never forget. Gretchen looks out of the peephole and sees Wendy, Eddy's fiancée. Panic washes over her as she realizes that she will be instrumental in destroying Wendy's hopes, dreams, and her perceived wonderful life. At that moment, Gretchen vows to help Wendy heal and find happiness.

"Hi, Wendy," Gretchen says, opening the door. "Please, come in."

Wendy shyly makes her way through the door carrying two Styrofoam cups of herbal tea. "I'm so sorry. I think I made a big mistake."

"Please, have a seat," Gretchen says, motioning to the table, and they sit down immediately. "So, what mistake did you make?"

"What happened to your eye?" Wendy asks. "That's bad."

"Long story for another time," Gretchen replies.

"Oh, here," Wendy says, placing a cup on the table in front of Gretchen. "I hope you like peppermint tea with honey. It's my favorite."

"I do. Thank you," Gretchen says and starts drinking her tea.

Wendy smiles, "Well, I know it was supposed to be a surprise, but I'm so excited about the bridal celebration you're planning; I mentioned it to Eddy. I don't understand everything, but for some reason, he got furious. Eddy said he doesn't want me to be friends with you. And he said a bunch of other stuff. But I have to tell you; I enjoy our time together. You may not know this, but I don't have many friends. I was starting to think of you as my best friend."

Gretchen already feels so guilty that she will give Wendy a shower. This encounter is tripling that guilt. She is also afraid that Wendy will marry Eddy even if he is in jail.

"Aaaawww. That's so sweet of you to say. I enjoy our time together, too," Gretchen says.

"I meant to ask you; I thought I saw Eddy's car in the parking lot. Is he here?"

A sinking feeling engulfs Gretchen. "There's something I have to tell you, too." She stares at the floor, trying to decide where and how to start. She finishes her tea to buy time. "Eddy may not be the person you think he is. He may have killed Kathleen Fitzgerald and several others that he's dated!"

"What? My Eddy, a killer? Never. He has flaws, and he can get outraged but never kill anybody. That's ridiculous. And I thought Kathleen Fitzgerald drowned?"

Gretchen is very concerned about Wendy; she is desperate to get through to her. She takes a deep breath and pulls up her left sleeve. "Look. He did this to me. Eddy did it to me! And he did the same thing to Kathleen Fitzgerald."

"Ugh. That looks nasty. And painful," Wendy says.

"Yes. And Eddy did this. And this!" Gretchen says, pointing to her eye.

"So, when did he make that scar?" Wendy asks.

"When we dated a long time ago," Gretchen answers.

"But wait. You told me you never dated Eddy. You said you were just friends. So, now who is it that I don't actually know?" Wendy asks and looks sternly at Gretchen.

Gretchen is trying to get her thoughts together. She is getting dizzy and thinks it must be from the choking.

"Do you know why Eddy burned you?" Wendy asks. "His mom had a scar just like that, from a fireplace accident. It was in the same place on her arm. When Eddy was little, his mom would cuddle with him, and he laid his head on her arm for a pillow. He would look at the different colors and shapes in the scar. Eddy always felt loved and safe there. He adored his mom. That's the main reason Eddy wanted to be a success; he bought his mom a house and supported her. Eddy never wanted her to work again because she worked so hard to raise him. Isn't that so sweet? Did Kathleen's scar look something like this?"

Wendy pushes up her shirt sleeve, revealing a similar scar. "The difference is, I let Eddy scar my arm. It meant so much to him," Wendy says, reflecting on that time. Then she says emphatically, "Oh, and Eddy could not have killed Kathleen. He was in Italy when she died."

"What?" Gretchen is very groggy, and her head is starting to spin.

"And he couldn't have killed Leslie because he was doing a photoshoot in Cancun when she fell over the balcony." Gretchen tries to stand and stumbles back in the chair. "So, it was you?" she slurs.

"Kathleen had too much of a hold on him. Oh, and she let Eddy scar her arm. I thought I was the only one to do that. I knew their affair would never stop. Eddy's mom's name was Kathleen. And I could never compete with the likes of Pamala or Carolyn. I know Eddy is marrying me because of my social standing, and I'm okay with that. Eddy told me you were just trying to cause problems for him and us. Oh, and by you dying when Eddy is with your friends proves he's not the killer. And with you gone, all this will die down. Pun intended. See, Eddy told me to wait in the car while he came in here. By the way, thank you for telling me about Littia. I didn't know about her. She told me about you bringing her orange juice. That's where I got the idea for the tea. Oh, and she's no longer a problem. Poor thing committed suicide."

Gretchen can't get up, and her slurring is worse. "Eddy is going to be so mad at you. Littia is the mother of his son!"

"What? Eddy has a son? I want to give him children."

"That tea. What was in it?" Gretchen frantically asks.

"Nothing you would know. But you've heard of poison darts, right? Well, different tribes use different poisons. I've spent a lot of time in the Orient, the Middle East, and Africa. This version takes longer to work when ingested instead of shot, but the chemical's half-life is much shorter. That's how long it stays in the body. So, it's hard to detect and trace. Which makes it hard to diagnose, and that comes in handy. And if they manage to come up with an answer, it will surprise you what they say. Although you won't be around to hear it, eh," Wendy says, grinning.

"You'll get caught."

"Sweet little ole me? I don't think so. Haven't yet."

"The po—li—ce...." Gretchen passes out, and her head falls to the table.

"Well, it's about time."

There is a knock at the door. "Ms. Crandall, open up, please."

Wendy panics. She grabs her purse, runs to the bedroom, and gets under the bed next to the headboard.

"Gretchen," Hamer yells and opens the door. Two plain-clothes detectives enter.

Chad runs to Gretchen and tries to rouse her. She doesn't move.

"We've got to get her to the hospital," Chad says, picking her up in his arms.

"I'll take you with the siren," Detective Murphy says.

They are making a lot of noise, so Wendy can settle in without being heard.

Chad runs to the unmarked car carrying Gretchen and yells, "Hamer, grab the cups!"

The detective puts the flashing light on the roof and takes off like the wind, with the siren blaring. He calls the hospital so that they will be expecting them. Hamer is right behind them with the cups.

The other detective radios headquarters from Gretchen's apartment. "Captain, I need you to send a couple more guys to the Crandall residence ASAP."

Chapter Twenty-Five

I See You

Chad and Hamer are both pacing the floor in the hospital.

"They're going to get her fixed," Hamer says, wringing his hands. "Georgetown is a great hospital! That's why we came here. It's excellent. And close. Johns Hopkins may be better, but it's too far."

"I hope so. Gretchen looks pretty bad and barely has a pulse!" Chad says, rubbing his neck.

In walk some people from the newspaper office. Hamer has called them all, and everyone is coming. As sometimes happens, co-workers become family, which is essential for everyone. They love Gretchen. People are leaving restaurants, dinner parties, dance clubs, and various other situations to get there. Of course, Lloyd is coming from the newspaper office, which, in reality, is his home.

Phyllis enters first, almost running. "How is she?" she asks Hamer. Anne, Charlotte, and Jill follow behind her.

"We're waiting to hear. It's bad. Gretchen's in terrible shape," Hamer says with tears in his eyes.

~~~

At Gretchen's apartment, Wendy tries to be as quiet as possible. She is doing a breathing technique she learned in India. It is prolonged and extremely silent.

The two officers that joined the detective are interviewing the neighbors to see if they saw or heard anything. Detective Garner scans the apartment and closets. He glances under the bed but does not see Wendy. She has some sweater bins concealing her at the top of the bed. The dusting for fingerprints process is in progress. The officers return to the apartment.

"Nobody saw or heard anything. Nothing. Nada," Officer Bowling reports.

"There has to be something in here to help us. We need to comb every inch," Detective Garner says.

"Yes, sir," the officers respond.

~~~

More co-workers have arrived at the hospital. Everyone is on one side of the waiting room. Katie, Beth, Ruth, and Barney are all talking to Hamer at once. Phyllis walks back from checking to see if there is any change in Gretchen's condition. She sees everyone gathered on the right side of the room, everyone except Lloyd. He is in a chair on the other side by himself. Lloyd is leaning forward with his elbows on his knees and his head in his hands. For the very first time ever, Phyllis feels sorry for him. She walks over and sits in the chair next to Lloyd.

"I tried to find out if there has been any change in Gretchen's condition, but they said to wait. Someone will be out to talk to us as soon as they have something to say," Phyllis says.

Lloyd is highly distraught. He looks at Phyllis. "This is all my fault! I should have given Gretchen better assignments. She deserved them. I think I was afraid if she got better assignments, she'd leave. And I don't want her to go—ever! I love that kid. I know she's not a kid, but to me, she's the closest thing to the daughter or granddaughter I never had. If anything happens to her…" Lloyd stops himself. He clears his throat. "Don't ever tell her—or anyone—what I said. *Ever*," he says, back to his gruff manner.

The whole group notices Phyllis and rushes over to her. "Did you find out anything?" Charlotte asks.

"No. We just have to wait till someone comes out to talk to us," Phyllis answers.

"Waiting is hard," Beth shakes her head. "Even if you're waiting for something good, like a baby to be born. But this is life and death stuff!"

"Yeah," Jill responds.

Phyllis is looking at the group. Then she sees Chad sitting by himself on the right side of the room, staring at the doors where the doctor will come out. "Good grief," Phyllis says as she stands, intending to go to Chad. At that moment, she sees Chad rushing toward the doors and the doctor that had just walked through them. Chad reaches the doctor first, followed by Phyllis and everybody.

"Are you with the Crandall case?" the doctor asks.

"Yes," Chad and Phyllis say at the same time while everyone else nods.

173

The doctor scans the group and proceeds. "We have ruled out stroke, heart attack, recreational drugs, and a myriad of other things. We've injected stimulants and gotten her blood pressure and heart rate up some, but they're still low. She is in a coma but is breathing on her own so far. We've gotten some bloodwork back but are still waiting on more. The lab is testing to see what possible poison or poisons she ingested. We are admitting her; she'll be in the Intensive Care Unit shortly. There is a waiting room outside the ICU. However, only one person can go in to see her at a time. And with her condition, we are limiting it to only two of you who can switch off. Whoever goes in will be covered totally in germ-free scrubs and a mask. We don't want to introduce germs or infectious material into her room that may further compromise her. You can wait here until she is in the ICU, or you can move to the ICU waiting room now. Tell the girl at the desk which you decide to do. We need to know where to find you should we need to."

The doctor starts to leave, and Chad asks. "How bad is she? What's her prognosis?"

"Comas are never good. Low stats are not good. We don't know what's causing her condition. I can't answer your questions definitively because we don't know where this is going," the doctor answers.

~~~

The apartment search continues. Officer Brown asks, "Do you want us to check the drawers?"

"Yes, everything!" Detective Garner replies.

By this time, Wendy has fallen asleep on her side. Officer Brown opens a drawer in the bedroom. Wendy wakes up with a start and hits her head on the bin in front of her.

"What was that? Does she have a pet? The noise came from under the bed," Brown says as the other two officers come into the room.

Wendy is petrified. They pull the bins out from under the bed and see her.

"Keep your hands visible and come out from under there. Or we'll pull you out," Garner says, pointing his gun at Wendy.

She slowly exits her hiding spot. "Is the guy gone?" Wendy asks in her shy, timid fashion.

Garner lowers his gun, and Brown helps her stand.

"What guy?" Garner asks.

"Gretchen's my best friend, and we were planning my bridal shower. This big guy, with brown hair and a black leather jacket, came in the door. They started yelling and fighting. I got scared and went under the bed. I've been there ever since. Who are you?" Wendy asks, in her timid way.

"Ah, the police," Brown says, pointing to his badge.

"We're going to need you to tell us everything you heard and, also, get you with our sketch artist," Garner says.

"I didn't hear much but noise because I kept my hands over my ears, like this." Wendy demonstrates in her fearful pretense.

~~~

At the hospital, everyone is sitting in the ICU waiting room. The nursing staff finishes connecting Gretchen to various monitoring devices. Phyllis knows how Gretchen feels about Chad and thinks he should be one of the ones going into the room. She also knows she is closer to Gretchen than anyone, and the SWAT team could not keep her out of that room. In her usual manner, Phyllis takes charge.

"Well, Chad, I think you and I should be the two to trade off going in to see Gretchen. Are you good with that?" she asks.

"Yes. Very much so. Thank you," Chad replies.

"Any objections?" Phyllis asks. Everyone just shakes their heads no. They all know when it comes to Gretchen and most everything else, Phyllis knows best.

"Hamer, would you please go to Gretchen's apartment? Look in her purse, and there's a small, zippered pouch with trinkets. Get the mustard seed and bring it here. And when you get back, please make a schedule for everyone alternating being at the hospital. People will need sleep and showers, or somebody else will end up sick," Phyllis says.

"Sure thing," Hamer responds and leaves the waiting room.

Phyllis continues, "Anne, Katie, Jill, and Ruth." They all walk to Phyllis. "You four are always talking about prayer, and you three are always talking about miracles. You know I don't much believe in such things. Now's your chance to prove me wrong. If we ever needed a miracle, this would be the time!" Phyllis says.

Chapter Twenty-Six

WE NEED EACH OTHER

Wendy has been working with the sketch artist for over an hour. She had already spent two hours at the police station giving her statement and going through mug shots on the computer. She is enjoying all the attention and the company.

One of the officers goes to talk to Detective Garner. "Sir, Eddy Osborne still says he has no idea who the guy that attacked Gretchen, other than himself, would be. He's clueless. And we believe him. What would he have to gain by not telling us? In his mind, it may take some of the heat off him," he says.

"Okay. Thanks for handling that," Garner says.

Detective Garner enters the room where the sketch artist and Wendy are working. "It's very late. Are you guys finished yet?" he asks.

"Yes. Just now," the artist answers and turns the drawing toward Garner so he can see it.

"Ah, wait. Doesn't that look like Chris Pratt in a leather jacket?" he asks.

The artist looks at the picture. "Well, yes. I guess it does," she says.

"Hmmm. Well, thank you, Wendy. You must be wanting to get home. We appreciate your help," Garner says.

"Oh, yes, sir," she answers, in all her sweetness, as she stands. "Anything to help catch Gretchen's killer. If you need something else, just let me know."

"Welp, he's not a killer yet, and let's hope it stays that way," Garner says.

"What do you mean?" Wendy asks.

"The last I heard, Gretchen's alive. She's still hangin' in," he says.

"What! Gretchen's alive!" she exclaims in anger and then tries to cover it as surprise.

With Wendy's untimid outburst, Detective Garner and the artist are shocked.

Wendy quickly goes into cover-up mode. "Oh, let's hope she makes it. I've got to get to the hospital to see her. Can you drive me there instead of home?" she asks, slipping back into her shy routine.

"We were going to drive you back to Gretchen's apartment complex to get your car," Garner says.

Wendy stammers, trying to think. Eddy has the keys to his car at the jail. She was in his car with him, so Wendy does not want to go back there and be stuck. She feels she has to get to the hospital as soon as possible.

"Oh, I took an Uber to Gretchen's. My car's not there," she says.

"Then I'll have an officer drive you home to get your car. Otherwise, you'll be stranded at the hospital," Garner replies.

Wendy quickly decides that is probably a good idea because she may need some things from her house or elsewhere. "Thank you," she says.

As soon as Wendy is gone, Garner goes to the lead officer. "Go see what you can get out of Eddy Osborne about Wendy Monroe. See if he knows anything. Something's just not smelling right," he says.

~~~

Barney, Charlotte, and Darla left the hospital first. According to Hamer's schedule, Lloyd should be gone, too. Hamer is having a hard time getting him to leave. He thinks he may have to wait until Phyllis gets out of the room with Gretchen because Lloyd will listen to her better than Hamer.

Phyllis is sitting next to Gretchen. She has her hand on Gretchen's arm. Phyllis cannot believe how bad Gretchen looks and how pale she has gotten. Earlier, Phyllis took the mustard seed charm off Gretchen's bracelet where Hamer found it. She has the encased mustard seed tied onto the side railing with a piece of string she got from the nurses' station. She hopes that Gretchen will see it as soon as she opens her eyes. Phyllis is sure it used to be a necklace because of the perfect hole holding the string. The nurse tells Phyllis she must leave for about twenty to thirty minutes. The staff has some work to do with Gretchen.

"How is she doing?" Phyllis asks the nurse as she stands to leave.

"About the same. She's no better, but she's no worse either. Right now, that's good," the nurse replies.

Phyllis joins the others in the waiting room. She gives them the latest report, no change. Hamer pulls Phyllis to the side and tells her about Lloyd not leaving. Overhearing the conversation, Chad joins them.

"Look," Chad says. "I don't blame him for not wanting to leave. I got each of us rooms at the Leavey Conference Center Hotel. It's right on the hospital campus. I got one for Lloyd, too. Oh, and a suite for the prayer ladies. I figured they'd want to stay together," he says.

"That's brilliant," Phyllis says. "Thank you so much. It's perfect and so helpful."

"And expensive," Hamer chimes into the conversation.

Phyllis whips her head around and glares at Hamer. "Money does not matter at a time like this! Bite your tongue, child!" she snaps.

Chad looks at Hamer. "What she said." He smiles and winks.

Phyllis moves on to immediately getting things done. "The way I see it, we need two people in the waiting room at all times. One to keep guard, in case we need to get everyone back here, heaven forbid—"

Hamer interrupts. "Wait. I didn't think you believe in Heaven?"

Phyllis huffs. "I said I'm not sure there is a Heaven. And as the old saying goes, 'There are no atheists in a foxhole.' And we're in a foxhole. The other person can nap. That way, we're covered. Chad, you can go in with Gretchen when they're done. I'm going to try to get Lloyd to his hotel room to sleep. I'll have him escort me. Thanks again for the rooms."

"Just give them the password *mustard seed* and my name, and they'll give you all the room keys," Chad says. "Oh, and it's set up, any food anyone wants, they can charge to their room number. It's taken care of. That goes for the cafeteria and gift shops, too."

"Thank you again," Phyllis says as she goes toward Lloyd.

"Hey, man," Hamer says, putting his hand on Chad's shoulder. "That's majorly decent."

The nurse walks into the waiting room. "Whoever is going in with Gretchen Crandall needs to get scrubbed and ready. We gave her some more adrenalin; hopefully, that will help," she says.

"That would be me," Chad says excitedly. He has so wanted to get back in with Gretchen; he rushes off with the nurse.

~~~

People are scurrying around the police station.

"Where are the lab reports?" Garner is yelling.

"They just got here, sir. Our lab and the hospital lab are working in tandem. They ran the tests three times because they weren't getting definitive results. The closest thing they can get from the one cup and the bloodwork is that its kind of like brown recluse spider venom," the officer says.

"What? Spider venom? Kind of? Keep the doctor and hospital in the loop," Garner instructs.

"They're trying to get the lab at NIH or Johns Hopkins to run it. Would you have any clout at the FBI lab?"

~~~

Chad is holding Gretchen's hand and stroking her cheek. He wishes he did not have to wear gloves. One of the nurses comes to check her vitals and gives Chad a funny look.

"Is this okay to do?" Chad asks.

"In coma situations, touching can be very helpful. Keep it up," the nurse says.

Hamer is keeping watch in the waiting room while Katie takes a nap. Tiptoeing, Wendy enters the waiting room. She walks to Hamer and explains that Gretchen is her best friend, inquiring who Hamer is and if he is there with Gretchen. Wendy asks when she can go in to see Gretchen.

"Not any time soon. Only Phyllis and Chad are allowed to take turns being there for now," Hamer says.

"But she's my BFF. I've got to see her," Wendy says and starts crying.

"Hey, look, lady, you've got to wait till Phyllis gets back. You can take it up with her," Hamer says emphatically.

Chad kisses the top of Gretchen's head wearing his mask. Then he kisses her forehead as he strokes her cheek again. For the first time, Gretchen moves her head slightly. A machine beeps.

The nurse quickly steps into the room. "Keep doing whatever you're doing!" she says.

Chad keeps stroking Gretchen's cheek, and he kisses the top of her head and forehead. Unexpectedly, Gretchen's hand moves. Alarms sound and Chad is startled.

Wendy hears the alarm and peeks around the nurses' station. She sees Gretchen's movement and panics!

~~~

An officer walks in with a stack of paperwork and goes to Detective Garner's office.

"Three things—One: Grasping at straws, the hospital says they have meticulously checked Crandall, and there is *no* sign of a spider bite anywhere on her body. That includes checking under each fingernail and toenail. They also microscopically studied the hair follicles on her scalp. Nothing.

"Two: The cups. One cup has Crandall's prints and Monroe's prints. That's the cup with the weird stuff. But the other cup with just the tea and honey only has Monroe's fingerprints. What's strange about that is Monroe said Crandall made the tea for them. Crandall's prints should be on Monroe's cup, too, if that's true.

"Also, number three: Eddy Osborne doesn't know anything about what Monroe has said. But he says that Wendy is his fiancée and she was waiting in his car for him."

"What? You should have started with number three. Send two guys to Crandall's hospital room and two to Monroe's house. And call the D.C. police immediately since the hospital is there. I want Monroe in custody *now!*" Garner demands.

~~~

Wendy is pleading with the nurse to see Gretchen. She will not stop, and the nurse will not relent. "But she's my best friend," Wendy says and then runs into Gretchen's room.

"Oh, Gretchen, you're okay. You had us all so worried," Wendy says in her ultra-sweet manner.

At the sound of Wendy's voice, Gretchen becomes very agitated. Two nurses come into the room with a security guard. "You've got to leave. You cannot be in here," they demand.

"Just let me hug her," Wendy says.

Holding the charm of her Egyptian bracelet in her hand, Wendy lunges at Gretchen. At the same time, Chad does a karate kick, sending Wendy sailing across the room.

Another hospital security guard enters the room with two D.C. police officers. They take Wendy into custody. She tries to drop her bracelet in a trashcan as they go down the hall, but the officers stop her.

The D.C. police captain calls the Maryland police captain. Being so close in vicinity, they often must cooperate on cases.

"Thanks for nabbing her guys. Be careful. Don't let her sweet and shy act fool you. She's bad! Please get that bracelet to the lab STAT. We're requesting an emergency search warrant for Monroe's car and house. She lives in Potomac, Maryland, so it's our jurisdiction. Makes it way easier," the captain says.

The D.C. police captain responds, "Well, we're keeping her locked up for now. It will be interesting to find out what's in that bracelet."

Hamer has summoned everyone, but Gretchen has not moved again. Chad strokes her hair and her face, gently kissing her forehead and hand.

The doctor enters the room and asks Chad to step out.

"What happened? She was moving. She was responding," Chad says franticly.

"That may be a good sign, or it may have been the adrenalin we gave her. We have to wait and see," the doctor says, motioning for him to leave.

Chad walks outside the door, waiting desperately to go back in with Gretchen.

Chapter Twenty-Seven

SUGAR AND SPICE AND LOTS OF NOT NICE!

Detective Garner is in the lab, and the lab technician explains what they have found.

"Sir, you've got to see this. When you push the jewel on the charm of this bracelet, it has a spring-loaded release that sends out a sharp pinpoint-type device. It delivers whatever liquid has been drawn inside of it. Right now, it has that same substance that is similar to the brown recluse spider venom mixed with other toxins we've been finding. But the pinpoint leaves a mark similar to a bee sting, not a spider bite. Let me tell you, this is one nasty, little dangerous device," the tech says.

"I've never seen anything like that. Have you?" Garner asks.

"No, and I'm glad about that. It's like something from the Dark Ages. I've seen poison rings in textbooks, but they just flip open and hold the poison. This is scary and even more diabolical. Evil keeps growing, I guess," the tech says.

"We know that for sure, with all we see," Garner responds.

"That's the truth!" the tech replies.

"I think they can easily hold Wendy on attempted murder," Garner declares. " 'Cause, that's what it is—no matter what kind of fancy lawyer she has. We're doing everything by the book. No mistakes that let her walk. We're heading over to execute the search warrant. We'll see what else we find."

Five detectives are searching Wendy's residence. Her parents are out of town for two more weeks, making it somewhat easier. They have been at it for hours but have yet to find anything until Detective Franco yells from the basement.

"Get down here, guys. Now," Franco yells.

They come running down the stairs. There is a door hidden behind a wall tapestry.

"We're going into this room together!" Franco declares.

They enter to find hundreds of glass canisters holding brown recluse spiders, black widow spiders, and species of spiders that they cannot identify. Larger aquariums hold numerous snakes, lizards, and creatures they have never seen. In addition, human skulls and bones are scattered everywhere.

"Well, I think we found what we were looking for. This place is creepy," Garner says.

"Yes, horror show creepy! I'm going to have nightmares for a week," Adams admits.

"We'll have the pros from the lab come here and figure this out," Garner says. "They'll get faster results."

Franco accidentally bumps open the lid of an aquarium. Rapidly, a giant snake bolts out of the container and quickly slithers across the floor toward Garner. Adams immediately shoots the snake twice.

"Thanks, man. What was that?" Garner asks.

"Not sure. No time to find out," Adams replies.

"Let's get the guys with the boots and suits in here. Time for us to go," Garner says.

~~~

Gretchen's condition has not changed since she made those slight, involuntary movements earlier. Phyllis is with her now, but she wants to get Chad back in the room since Gretchen responded when he was there. Phyllis is holding Gretchen's hand and stroking her hair. She is following Chad's pattern, hoping for more positive results.

Earlier, while the nurses were bathing Gretchen, the prayer ladies—as Chad calls them—had everyone join them for a group prayer. Lloyd and Phyllis were slightly uncomfortable with it, but everybody else was good. When they were alone, Lloyd told Phyllis, "I have to admit, I'm not uncomfortable because I don't believe. I grew up going to church and continued well into my twenties. But then I got busy with my career and life and bad habits. So, I'm uncomfortable because I feel guilty. I wonder if I had kept going, would I have a family and kids, and even grandkids now?"

Phyllis is thinking about that conversation while stroking Gretchen's hair. Then she trades places with Chad and goes back to the waiting room with Lloyd.

Chad is stroking Gretchen's hair. Suddenly, she raises her hand, and it looks like she is trying to touch the mustard seed. A slight smile comes on her face. Then her hand drops, and her smile fades. Alarms begin to scream, and her heart monitor has a flatline and has a constant tone. Nurses and doctors come running into the room and push Chad out of the way. Chad is terrified and moves over for the crash cart to enter.

He knows what this means. Everyone from the waiting room peeks to see who is in trouble. The prayer ladies rush to the corner of the waiting room, fall to their knees, and immediately and fervently pray. Moments later, struggling to kneel, Lloyd joins them. He has tears streaming down his face.

~~~

"Garner, you will not believe all the poisonous stuff they've found in that room," the captain says. "Stuff I've never heard of, and they're still working. Some of the snakes and spiders shouldn't even be in this country. We think they had to be flown in by private plane and kept concealed. By the way, it's a good thing Adams shot that snake that was after you. It was a black mamba. Can easily be deadly!"

"It was so eerie in that room; it was like you could feel the evil," Garner replies, his voice trembling. "And you know we've seen horrible stuff. Dead bodies mutilated and worse! You should see how sweet and innocent this woman acts. You won't believe it."

"So, I've heard," the captain says. "The pros are still identifying creatures. We know that there are brown recluse spiders, black widows, funnel-web spiders. Even something called a camel spider. It's majorly nasty, ugly, and big. They can be six inches long and can run up to ten miles per hour. But it isn't even a spider at all. It's known as the wind scorpion. Also, they found a Mozambique spitting cobra, and the list keeps growing. The entire lab staff is working overtime as fast as possible to save Crandall. They think it's a concoction of venoms."

Garner grits his teeth. "How about you put me in a room with Wendy Monroe for five minutes and no cameras. I'll get you the venom concoction in precise percentages—*fast*." Garner pounds his right fist into his left palm unconsciously.

"She's already lawyered up. It's a nightmare. Somehow, we've got to nail her. I just hope Crandall makes it," the captain says.

~~~

A doctor walks into the waiting room to talk to Gretchen's group. "We were able to get her heart started, and, for now, she's stable. Mr. Fitzgerald's with her. We don't want her to be alone. We've been waiting to try specific anti-venom treatments without the toxins definitively identified. However, with this latest episode, we administered anti-venom for brown recluse. It was too dangerous to wait any longer. We'll keep you advised," he says, returning to the ICU.

Chad is stroking Gretchen's hair and her cheek gently. She is very pale. He is highly concerned and knows he would give everything he has to make her well. However, money cannot fix many things in life, as well he understands—especially pains of the heart. Chad kisses the top of Gretchen's head and then her forehead. In a moment of desperation, Chad clutches the mustard seed tied to the bed railing.

~~~

Adams rushes into Garner's office. "Man, you've got to see this briefing from the lab. We're lucky we got out of that place alive! There is some freaky stuff," he says, going back to the evidence room. Garner is close behind.

In the evidence room, officers are watching the large screen for briefings. The head of the lab is giving the presentation. She is showing each type of snake and providing a detailed description. "I want you to pay close attention because we don't know what's out there," she explains. "Any of what you are about to see could be, so you need to be very smart and highly cautious. You will know some of what you are about to see and hear, but there is a lot you will never have heard of.

"Starting with the snakes, a king cobra bite can kill an elephant in less than three hours. If not treated, its bite is fatal in humans 50-60% of the time. The western or inland taipan is related to the cobra but is even more deadly. It has an 80% death rate for humans if untreated. It releases a mix of poisons: neurotoxins, procoagulants, mycotoxins that inhibit breathing, cause hemorrhaging in tissues and blood vessels, paralyzing and damaging muscles. The banded krait is also related to the cobra but is highly venomous and causes paralysis. This next one is even creepier. The boomslang resembles a stick or a branch and waits to attack. Unlike other snakes, it has rear fangs and chews its victims until it delivers enough toxins to kill. The black mamba has venom that is exceptionally potent, killing humans often. The barba amarilla is often deadly, with painful and necrotizing venom. This next snake probably kills more people than all other snakes combined. The saw-scaled viper, biting early and frequently. It's the repetitive biting that makes it so deadly.

"You cannot be too vigilant. It's a dangerous time, and we need to help save each other, the way Officer Adams did for Officer Garner. Some of these snakes can stay hidden for a very long time. There's more, but we'll take a break. Be back in five."

Garner looks at Adams. "More! Like that isn't enough. Thanks again for taking that shot. I owe you, man," he says to Adams.

"Nah, that's just what we do," Adams says, patting Garner's back.

~~~

A nurse rushes in, followed by a doctor. The nurse grabs Chad's arm. "Come with me," she says, pulling him out of Gretchen's area. "They've identified three more toxins. We're finally getting somewhere! Dr. Davidson is administering pure hope as we speak!" she says.

Phyllis and the rest of the crew are climbing the walls with anxiety. They take turns eating in the cafeteria, but Phyllis has taken up Gretchen's bad emotional eating habit. She hits the candy machine for something sweet, then the snack machine for something salty and crunchy.

"I finally understand why she does it," Phyllis says, handing Lloyd a bag of chips. "It helps. It may not solve anything, but it is a stress reliever. I'll go on a diet when we get through this." Chuckling, she jabs Lloyd. "Hey, we can start taking a walk together during lunch; what say?"

"First, I'd have to start taking lunch, which I never do," Lloyd replies.

"And that's one of the things we need to change," Phyllis says emphatically.

"Maybe we should have a group prayer," Lloyd suggests. "That's got to help more than chocolate, caramel, pretzels, or chips."

"Good idea," Phyllis says, not knowing if he genuinely wants prayer or just for her to be quiet.

Chapter Twenty-Eight

HEARTS AND HANDS

Adams groans and looks at Garner. "Who knew there were so many haunting things in the world. I said I would be having nightmares for a week. Make it months."

The briefing continues. "Okay, people, we're almost finished," the head of the lab says. "I know this has been a lot to take in. One more spider, and we'll call it quits. Number ten— the Brazilian Wandering Spider is usually on banana leaves or bunches. Poisonous to humans. It causes salivation, irregular heartbeat, and *painful*, long-lasting erections. They have even tested its venom for treating erectile dysfunction. It hasn't worked, but they've tried." She pauses a moment as everyone chuckles. "Keep alert. Keep safe. Take action. Remember: Early treatment saves lives."

Garner looks at Adams. "As creepy as all this stuff is, what scares me the most is that woman, Wendy! All the snake and spider junk, that's nature and instinct. She is all *choice* and *pure evil* in my book! I'm just saying; I think *she should* be giving you nightmares."

~~~

Dr. Davidson enters the waiting room. He goes directly to Phyllis and Lloyd, pulling over a chair and sitting. The others move closer so they can hear.

"Outstanding news," he says. "The labs, several of them cooperating, have identified seven different toxins that were combined that have been working in tandem to kill Ms. Crandall. We have performed countermeasures to reverse all the effects that we can. Positive results are happening. Ms. Crandall's heart rate is up. Her blood pressure has improved, and, most importantly, we see increased brain function."

Everyone is smiling, excited, and hugging. The doctor clears his throat, and they all quieten.

Dr. Davidson continues. "She is not out of the woods yet. But I have to tell you, the fact that she is doing as well as she is, is nothing less than remarkable. The whole staff is talking about it. Some believe that there is more at work here than just medicine. Truthfully, I'm one of them. She was in bad shape. Let's hope it keeps going well," he says, standing to leave.

"Thank you so much. We all needed some good news," Phyllis says with a huge smile.

Dr. Davidson smiles and goes back to the ICU.

"Now, we have a group prayer of thanksgiving," Jill says. "Everybody asks God for things, but many forget to thank Him."

"Then we'll have a prayer asking for Gretchen's full recovery," Katie adds.

Phyllis looks at the prayer ladies and smiles. "Girls, I may not believe everything you believe, but I promise you one thing," she says, pointing her finger at each of them. "I will never make fun of you again."

~~~

Garner and Adams are in the captain's office. "Captain, I think we need to get some bodies exhumed. I don't think Gretchen is the first person this woman has tried to kill. With her arsenal of poisons and concoctions, she could make accidents or injuries or illnesses all look natural, when in fact, they're murder!" Garner says with indignation.

"Well, you may be right. Get me facts," the captain says. "Investigate everything regarding Wendy Monroe for the last five years. We'll start with that and go from there. I'm putting you two on all aspects of this case full time and making it a top priority. She had to be doing something with all those poisons. And see if anybody else was involved—a chemist or something. The lab said that not only was she mixing poisons, but she was trying to get different species to mate and create new and deadlier predators. She seems evil, but she doesn't seem that smart."

~~~

Chad is holding Gretchen's hand and stroking her hair. Gretchen's head starts moving, and her eyes slowly open. Chad freezes. At first, she has trouble focusing. She tries licking her lips, but her mouth is dry.

"Is that you, Chad? Or am I dreaming?" she asks.

"Yes, it's me, Gretchen. I'm right here with you. You're not dreaming. It's real," Chad says, with his eyes starting to tear. He dabs her lips with the moisturizing glycerin swab the nurse gave him. "This should help your lips," he says.

There is an alarm beeping from Gretchen's head movement. A nurse rushes into the room.

"Well, sleeping beauty, are you waking up? It's good to see those pretty eyes," the nurse says with a big smile. "We've all been pulling for you, especially this guy." The nurse takes a small flashlight from her pocket and checks both of Gretchen's eyes. "Looking good. Now, squeeze my hands as hard as you can," she says, taking Gretchen's hand from Chad. "Sorry, I need both of them. Hard. Harder. Good job. It's nice to have you back with us."

Gretchen smiles and tries to reach for Chad. He takes her hand. "I'm here. Right here," he says, kissing her hand, then her head, and stroking her cheek, the same way he had been doing while she was asleep.

As the nurse with Gretchen finishes gathering data, another nurse goes to the waiting room.

"Ms. Crandall is awake!" the nurse announces. Everyone is ecstatic. "I just got off the phone with the doctor. He will let all of you step to the nursing station, so you aren't too close, but Ms. Crandall can see you. But you have to be very quiet. We have other patients, and some are sleeping. You can only stay a minute. But seeing everybody will help with her recovery. Feeling loved is great medicine."

They all nod and follow the nurse. She motions for them to stop, forming a line in front of the nurses' station. The nurse quietly pushes Gretchen's curtain back to see her friends.

The nurse smiles. "There are some people here who are anxious to see you. But don't try to sit up or say anything. They just want you to know they love you and have been here for you."

Everyone is waving. Jill and Charlotte blow kisses, and others join in. Some are sending hugs. Hamer makes a heart with his hands, then they all make hand hearts. The nurse gives two thumbs up and motions for them to leave. Gretchen is smiling and feels very loved. Tears fill her eyes. She is also very frail. As the doctor enters, Chad kisses Gretchen's head and her hand. He steps out, and the curtains close behind him. Chad fights back tears.

Chad enters the waiting room. Everybody is crying. There are tears of joy, relief, and some tears of exhaustion. Relatives of another patient in the waiting area are not sure if someone is living or dying. Chad chuckles. He has never seen so much love. Phyllis walks over to Chad.

"Grand job helping her to wake up," she says and gives him a huge hug. "But now it's my turn to go in." They both laugh.

After a short while, some people are getting ready to leave. It has been a long, exhausting ten days. They want to be home. Barney and Charlotte announce they are leaving and start saying their goodbyes.

Lloyd jumps up and begins speaking in a gruff voice. "Not so fast. Nobody goes anywhere until we have…" he pauses and looks at Jill. "What did you call it? Oh yeah, a prayer of thanksgiving. That's the least we can do after The Big Guy saved our Gretchen!" Lloyd says, with deep sincerity and fighting back the tears.

They all hold hands, bow their heads, and Lloyd says, "You're up, Jill."

Chapter Twenty-Nine

WOW!

Adams enters Garner's office with a bag of donuts and sits. "I think I got a brilliant idea while I was waiting in line at the donut drive-thru. It's funny; I never get ideas when I go inside but often do while waiting in the car. Never mind. Remember the evil woman, Eddy Osborne's fiancée?" Adams says.

Garner nods. "Yeah, Wendy Monroe."

"I can't think of her as 'Wendy.' It sounds too nice. You don't get the kind of nightmares I'm having from nice. Did you ever notice how close *evil* and *devil* are? I wonder if they started out saying 'da evil' and it turned into the 'devil'?" Adams says.

"You didn't get much sleep last night, did you?" Garner asks.

"No. I told you, these nightmares are bad!" Adams says.

"You were talking about Monroe," Garner reminds him.

"Why don't we see what names and info we can get from Eddy regarding Wevil? Hey, that's what I'm going to call her.

And maybe he could get her to tell some stuff, like confess some crimes," Adams says.

"That is a good idea," Garner says. "But question. Would that be *Wevil* like *evil* or *Wevil* like the *devil*?" Garner asks.

"Ah, man, don't mess with me," Adams says with a scowl.

"I'm not. That's a serious question. I think you have a good point," Garner says. "Either that, or we both need sleep."

"Let's go talk to Osborne. We can decide on the way," Adams says, grabbing the bag of donuts.

~~~

Gretchen is doing wonderfully. She can move, even though her mobility is limited. They have her sitting up at times, and her appetite is returning. The doctor transferred her to the step-down unit. If she continues to improve at this rate, she will be transferred to a regular room and start rehab.

Everybody went home that first night she was awake except for Phyllis, Chad, Lloyd, and Hamer. They are all still there. Now she can have two in the room at a time. So, they are taking turns of two. Gretchen loves them being there. However, she would like some alone time with Chad and, also, with Phyllis. She has things she wants to tell her.

Gretchen longs for Chad to hold her hand again. He has not been doing that with the others around, although he still kisses the top of her head each time he leaves.

Gretchen gasps. "I need to talk to the police," she says, with a stunned look on her face.

"What is it?" Phyllis asks.

"I just remembered Wendy confessing to other murders the night she tried to kill me. I guess she figured I'd be dead and not able to tell," Gretchen says, panicked.

Phyllis touches Gretchen's arm. "The doctor told us not to ask you any questions about anything. He said it's important for you to remember things on your own. It's part of your brain healing," she says.

"We'll get someone from the police to come to talk to you," Hamer says. "Are you sure you are up for it?"

"Yes. I want to get this out of my head. I don't like remembering it," Gretchen replies with a distressed look. "It's awful!"

"Okay, then. I'll take care of it. I have all my contacts on my computer in my room. I'll be back," Hamer says as he leaves in a rush.

"Thanks," Gretchen responds.

As soon as Gretchen can hear Hamer's footsteps down the hall, she looks at Phyllis. "While we can, we've got to talk. I've wanted to tell you what happened."

"What happened when," Phyllis asks.

"I think I died," Gretchen says.

"*What?* What do you mean?" she asks.

"Well, bells were going off, and I floated up out of my body. I could see Chad holding my hand and me lying there. The nurses came running in, and I left. I went to the waiting room. I saw you sitting with Lloyd, something I never thought I'd see. And I saw other people from the office.

"At that moment, this bright light came shining down from above like there was no ceiling there. It opened to the Heavens. It was amazing! Then I started floating into the light.

It felt great and was all warm, like being in the sunshine on a beautiful day, only a thousand times better.

"The next thing I knew, my Gramma was there! She hugged me and held me for a long time. I never wanted to leave. But she told me I couldn't stay; I had to come back. She said I have things I need to do. I said I miss her so much. She told me she misses me too but that we will be back together one day. But not now. Not yet.

"She said I'm going to get married and have three children, two girls and a boy. She highly recommends adopting a fourth child to eliminate the middle-child syndrome. She said it would help all the children and the whole family. Gramma's like that—she knows a lot of stuff. I tried to get her to tell me who I'm going to marry, but she wouldn't tell. She said I have to find that out for myself. She told me, 'Just marry a good man, and everything else will take care of itself.' Then I felt myself being pulled down. She said, 'It's time to go. *Jesus does love you—LOTS,* and I love you through the Universe and beyond. Forever.' I said, 'I love you through the Universe and beyond. Forever, too.'

"There was a small woosh, and I couldn't see her anymore. But I heard her say, 'Tell them the prayers helped.' I don't know what that meant. Then there was a big woosh, and I was sucked back into my body. I didn't want to be, but I was. It was incredible! Words don't do it justice," Gretchen says, glowing.

Phyllis is stunned. She doesn't know what to do or what to say. Gretchen was right. Phyllis was sitting next to Lloyd. Phyllis never thought she would see that either. Phyllis tries to tell herself that Gretchen had had an illusion, or it was a dream. However, how would Gretchen know she was sitting with Lloyd? Also, Gretchen does not know about the prayers. Phyllis is speechless, something that never happens.

Finally, Phyllis manages to say, "Wow!"

Hamer walks into the room. "They have two guys on the way. They're tremendously interested in what you have to say. They will record you. Everything you say is important. It needs to be exact," Hamer says.

Gretchen puts her hands on her cheeks. "Hamer, could you please get Chad here fast? I need to talk to him before the police come. I've got to ask him something vital," she says.

"Sure thing," Hamer replies.

Hamer calls and finds Chad in the cafeteria. He comes immediately to Gretchen's room.

Hamer says, "I'll step out, so there's only two."

"Ah, I need both of you to step out for a few minutes, please," Gretchen requests, looking at Phyllis and Hamer.

"No problem," Phyllis says, grabbing her purse and Hamer's arm.

As they leave, Gretchen motions Chad closer and speaks quietly. "I haven't had a chance to tell you. I just remembered it. Wendy killed Kathleen! Not Eddy. He was in Italy when Kathleen died. She confessed that to me and some other murders. The police are on the way to take my statement. Can I tell them about Kathleen's murder? Since it's not common knowledge, I won't say anything if I shouldn't. I'll only tell them about the other murders," she says.

Chad is dumbfounded. He pauses and is quiet for a few moments. "Of course, you can tell them. We were just keeping it quiet to help catch the killer. And you've done that. I'm sure they'll know what to keep confidential as they collect the evidence. Yes. Please, tell them," he says, somewhat in shock.

Chad stares out of the window for a short time. Gretchen stays quiet. He turns to Gretchen, "It's a relief to know who killed Kathleen. That's a heavy weight lifted off my shoulders. Thank you," he says.

"We'll talk more when we can. I know this is hard for you," Gretchen says. Purposely changing the subject, she continues, "By the way, did I tell you that John Adams is my second favorite Founding Father. He did some incredible stuff. And he never owned any slaves. Neither did his son, John Quincy Adams. John Adams was our second president, and his son was our sixth. However, the son is not one of the Founding Fathers, of course. What heroes these men are." She knows she is babbling a bit, trying to get through an uncomfortable spot.

Hamer walks in with the detectives. Detective Murphy drove Gretchen to the hospital, although she does not know that. He greets Chad, which puts Chad somewhat at ease. He is glad to know Murphy will be taking the info. The other is Detective Blare. They immediately get right to business.

"Thank you so much for doing this, Ms. Crandall," Detective Murphy says. "We know it's not easy, especially since you have not completely recovered. We will make the process as painless and quick as possible. If you need or want to stop at any time, don't hesitate to tell us. We'll either take a break or come back another time."

Hamer says to Chad, "That's our cue to leave." As he and Chad head for the exit, Hamer smiles at Gretchen. "We'll be right down the hall in the sitting area if you need us."

Gretchen tells the two detectives everything. She wants all of the information in their hands and out of her thoughts. Gretchen tells all the details about Kathleen and what Wendy had said, including the scars and the particulars of Eddy's mother. She relates about the girl named Leslie who fell over the balcony, seemingly because she was drunk. But her death had been aided in some form by Wendy. Eddy was in Cancun during this time. She also knows there are two other girls, Pamala and Carolyn, but she does not know the details regarding them. She relates every fact she can remember.

"This is a lot. You've been very accommodating. Thank you so much. Here's our card if you think of anything else," Detective Blare says.

Detective Murphy looks at Gretchen and just says, "Wow!"

Chapter Thirty

TRUTH IS FREEING

Garner and Adams have tracked Eddy to his house. Eddy made bail and still cannot believe he was arrested, spending time in jail, as well. His arrest will not suit the social standing that he has worked so hard to achieve. Plus, this is not a quasi-acceptable, white-collar crime. According to the socialites, the only thing terrible about that is getting caught. His offense is the low-class, hands-dirty kind of crime that nobody that is anyone would ever do. Oh, they may hire it done, but never would they do it themselves. Anyone with any status whatsoever avoids these people altogether. What is Eddy to do?

Adams rings the doorbell. When Garner and Adams explain that Eddy's assistance and cooperation with information on Wendy's criminal acts may improve his case, he is eager to help.

~~~

Gretchen is moved to a regular room. With each move, she has Phyllis tie the mustard seed onto her railing the way Phyllis initially had done. Gretchen is going to physical therapy in the mornings and rehabilitation in the afternoons. Both activities are exhausting for her.

Finally, Gretchen has managed to talk Lloyd and Hamer into returning to work. Keeping the office running via phone is not the same as being there. Nor is fulfilling assignments. They can visit her in the evenings. Lloyd is willing to do that because Phyllis is staying during the day. No one knows, but Lloyd is still paying Phyllis her salary to stay at the hospital. Of course, she would be there anyway but receiving her pay certainly helps.

The wheelchair enters the hospital room bringing Gretchen back from physical therapy. They make her travel by wheelchair because she is wobbly on her feet. She gets back in bed.

"They weren't exaggerating when they said those toxins take a lot out of you," Gretchen admits. "I feel like I've run a marathon. Well, to be more precise, I think this is how I'd feel after running a marathon. I've never run one, so I don't know."

"It's okay. I get it," Phyllis responds. "Listen, I keep thinking about what you told me happened with your Gramma. I can't stop thinking about it. Anyway, Chad's a good guy. What do you think?"

"I think Chad's fantastic. But remember Gramma wrote me some letters of wisdom to be opened at certain times because she wasn't here to help me. And she taught me some good stuff too. I remember what she told me. She's a smart lady, and now I'm paying more attention to all the things she tried to teach me over the years. She always said that any feelings we bury or 'stuff' haunt and control us our whole lives, or at least until we recognize and face them. She always said our reaction to an experience has more to do with our past than the current circumstances.

"I watched that when I was in middle school. Two girls would have completely different reactions to the same event. It was fascinating to see. Gramma and I would try to figure out what could have happened in their past to account for their different responses. It was fun. The point is, Chad has unfinished business and lots of emotional baggage to deal with before he can ever have a healthy relationship. Oh, and I need to work on myself too," Gretchen replies. "Plus, he doesn't hold my hand at all anymore. I don't know what happened. Maybe it was only sympathy."

~~~

Detective Murphy gave Adams and Garner the information Gretchen had provided. They are keeping Eddy uninformed. They do not want him to blow this opportunity by saying something he should not.

Eddy is preparing to visit Wendy in the D.C. prison. Garner is getting him wired. Using wires works better than remote transmission with all the metal in prison. Two D.C. policemen are helping them. Eddy's hair is long enough to place a tiny earpiece inside his ear canal, so they can communicate with him if necessary. They do not even want the guards to know Eddy is working with them.

"Now, Eddy, we want you to concentrate on Wendy's attack on Gretchen. See what you can get out of her. In general, being nice, being flattering, positive exchanges work much better than negative ones. We're only going to leave you in there for about fifteen minutes. It's just the initial contact. We need to do this in stages. Get her feeling comfortable. She will talk more freely if she trusts you. Do you think you can do it?" Garner asks.

"Piece of cake," Eddy responds. "Making females feel comfortable is my specialty. How do you think I've gotten so many compromising photos over the years?" he says, with a devilish grin.

Garner is putting the electronics pieces back in the case. Adams whispers to him, "Looks like he and Wevil are a good match. Or more accurately, a bad match!" he chuckles.

Wendy is excited that Eddy is coming to see her. The guards, as instructed, told her she would be having a visitor and who would be coming. She has been primping for hours, as much as she can in jail. She hates having to wear the drab prison garb. It is very unflattering. Also, she has had to pinch her cheeks for color, since she has no blush. She has even practiced her smile in the mirror.

The guard retrieves Wendy from her cell. She is so enthusiastic; she is practically dancing down the halls with an enormous smile. It is counter to the shy, timid persona she has been portraying. The surveillance cameras are filming it all. She enters the room and sits at the table. Wendy and Eddy will be as close as allowed. The detectives want the meeting to be as intimate as possible.

Eddy enters the room with the guard. Eddy sits at the table across from Wendy. She is so thrilled; she can hardly contain herself.

The guard says, "There will be absolutely *no* physical contact, as instructed. That means no touching whatsoever. I will remain with you the entire time. I will give you a two-minute warning before your time is up." He takes a step back.

"Oh, I knew you'd come. I just knew it! I want to touch you so much," Wendy says, gripping her hands to keep from touching Eddy.

Eddy is looking at Wendy like she has somewhat lost her mind. They do not have a passionate relationship, and he has never seen so much emotion from her.

"So, how's it goin'?" Eddy asks.

Adams turns to Garner in their listening room with the mike on mute. "This is the guy that's supposed to be so good with women. 'How's it goin'?' She's in jail, for Pete's sake. We're in trouble," he says.

Wendy smiles. "My attorney's trying to get me out on bail, but there are some issues with things they found at the house. It'll just take some time. He's super good. But I've been thinking, and I've got it all figured out. Even if I go to prison, we can go ahead and get married. Then, we'll get conjugal visits so we can start our family. I know how badly you want children. We can have a kid like every year or two. We'll hire a good nanny—an old grandmotherly type—so it won't interfere with your work and travel for shoots. How does that sound?" she says.

Eddy's jaw has dropped. He is unsure of what to say and sits in silence, looking at Wendy. "Well, did you try to kill Gretchen? And did you use poison?" he asks.

Wendy looks sweetly at Eddy. "Oh, that was for us. You said she was trying to cause trouble, and you didn't want me being friends with her. That just solved the problem," she says in her sweet, innocent voice. "You said you wanted her gone."

"Yeah. To Rhode Island, California, Arizona. Someplace else. *Not dead.* You don't just kill people because they're in your way. Or because they bother you," he says gruffly.

Wendy looks sad, and tears come to her eyes.

Garner grimaces. "Not going so well. Should we go for broke?" he asks, and Adams nods yes.

Garner turns on his mike. "Eddy, ask her about killing Kathleen Fitzgerald."

"What? Did you kill Kathleen? I thought she drowned. You couldn't have. I loved her," Eddy grimaced.

Wendy starts crying. "Yes. And that's why she had to die. You're supposed to love *me*! *Just me!*" she says, with clenched teeth.

Chapter Thirty-One

Jeweled and Bedazzled

Eddy sits in stunned silence. He cannot comprehend or believe that Wendy killed Kathleen. Garner comes to his rescue.

"Eddy, stay calm. Tell her you'll be back soon. Time's up, and you have to go. Eddy, do you hear me?" Garner asks.

"Time's up," Eddy says, standing slowly. "I'll be back soon."

"But the guard didn't say anything," Wendy says. "I don't want you to go!"

"Yes, he did. You just didn't hear him," Eddy says and looks at the guard. "Time's up, right?"

The guard looks at Eddy. "Yes. You've got to go," he says, instinctually agreeing with Eddy.

"When? When will you be back?" she asks.

Garner responds, "Later today, if they'll let me."

Eddy parrots what Garner told him, and the guard escorts him out of the door.

"I love you, Eddy! See you soon," Wendy shouts.

Eddy does not respond. He just keeps walking. Adams and Garner meet him down the hall.

"Did Wendy kill Kathleen? And who is that woman? I've never seen Wendy act like that," Eddy says, in a bit of shock.

"Come with us," Adams says. They take Eddy into a conference room. "Have a seat. Do you want a drink? Soda, water, coffee?"

"Water," Eddy replies as he sits in a chair. Garner pulls over a stool next to Eddy and turns it toward him. He sits, straddling the stool. Adams gets water from the small refrigerator in the corner and joins them.

"It is a definite possibility that Wendy did kill Kathleen. We're not sure. Kathleen's husband is permitting us to exhume the body. We need to do some testing," Garner says.

"That's insane. It can't be!" Eddy says emphatically.

Adams rubs Eddy's shoulder. "We need your help with several situations, it seems. Do you know someone named Carolyn that died? And someone named Pamala?" he asks.

"Yeah. I knew both the girls," Eddy replies.

Garner slides a legal-size pad of paper and pen to Eddy. "Please write down everyone you can think of that has died in the last five years and the circumstances of their death. Make that the last ten years," Garner says, looking at Adams.

~~~

Different people from the newspaper office have come on various nights to the hospital, but Lloyd and Hamer come every night. There are no restrictions on the number of visitors in Gretchen's current room. Some days she wishes there were because she still gets exhausted, even though she is doing re-remarkably better.

Lloyd comes into Gretchen's room and pulls up his chair. "You look outstanding," he says. "Not all pale and peaked like you were. You had me terrified there for a while. Well, I've decided to make you a promise. When you can come back to work, I will never, and I mean never, send you to cover a basket-weaving contest again." They all laugh.

Hamer asks Lloyd, "Hey man, how about getting us all some fries? The walk to the cafeteria will be good for you." Hamer turns to Gretchen, "Fries sound good, right?"

Gretchen knows Hamer well enough to know that that move translates to he has something to tell her. "Fries sound yummy," she says.

"On my way," Lloyd responds.

As soon as Lloyd is out of hearing range, Hamer begins. "I can't say this in front of Lloyd because he'll think it's too much on you. But I think it will be good for you to hear they're getting somewhere.

"Well, you know they found Littia dead after drinking vodka and taking sleeping pills. She left a suicide note. It said she couldn't take the guilt of lying to her husband and children anymore. Her youngest son belongs to someone else. The note was typed but not signed. With the alcohol and drug evidence right there, they weren't looking any further since there were only her fingerprints. Until that is, you talked to Detective Murphy. The coroner had not seen anything suspicious. Of course, at that time, he wasn't looking. It seemed cut and dry. Well, Littia was already in the ground, but they hadn't covered the coffin with dirt yet. They then investigated more. On the back of her scalp, two small puncture wounds were hard to see under her hair. Ends up, a banded krait had bitten her, which causes paralysis. They think the vodka and pills were forced into her stomach through a tube. It took time for everything to digest. Littia was alive this whole time but couldn't move! Probably had to listen to Wendy yap while she was dying. Isn't that awful?" Hamer says.

Gretchen is sitting with her hands on her cheeks and her mouth agape. "That's horrifying!" she responds.

Lloyd walks into the room with a tray of fries. "Did I give you enough time to talk with me gone?" he asks with a big grin.

~~~

"It's been two days since Eddy saw Wendy. Do you think she's rattled enough to break?" Garner asks Adams.

"My concern is Eddy. He's almost as looney as she is. We don't want him blowing our case, and we don't want him providing material for the lawyer to get her off with an insanity plea. She's more manipulative, selfish, and evil than she is insane. We do *not* want her walking or ending up at some cushy asylum for the rich," Adams says adamantly.

"I agree," Garner says. "But the prosecutor wants more evidence. He says he can see outs on what we have. It beats me how, but that's his job."

"Well, then, I guess we have to try Eddy. He's our only shot right now. I just hope we don't regret it," Adams replies.

Even though they have reservations, they make arrangements for Eddy to meet with Wendy again. They explain how important his role is and that this will get justice for Kathleen. He is wired and ready.

Eddy walks into the visiting room at the jail and sits down at the table. "I'm so happy to see you," Wendy says. "What took you so long?" she asks, hugging his hand to her chest.

"No touching," the officer says sternly.

Wendy lets go quickly. "I'm so sorry," she says.

"Officer, could you please give us some privacy?" Eddy asks.

"I can step over here, but that's as far as I can go," the officer replies and moves.

"Thank you," Eddy says and turns to Wendy. He looks directly at her and speaks softly. "If we are going to continue our relationship, I need you to tell me the truth. And I mean all of it—one chance. *Now*," he says firmly.

Wendy's eyes get big. She loves the idea that Eddy cares and wants to know. "Of course, I'll tell you anything and everything you want to know. I love you," she replies.

"How many people have you killed? Exactly. How many?" he asks and listens intently.

"I'll need your help to answer that accurately. I need you to go to my house. There's a key under the tallest frog statue by the pond. There's a jewelry box on my dresser. Count the number of jewels stuck to the top. How many jewels are there will be the number of people I've killed," she says and looks at Eddy lovingly.

"You mean that you've killed so many, you've lost count?" he says in a stern voice.

"You said I only have one chance, so I want to be certain. I can give you a guestimate if that's okay. And we can get married, and I can tell you all about each one. When you're my husband, they can't call you to testify against me," she says enthusiastically. "At least I think that's right. Oh, and I found out about Daddy paying you off twice before. That's not going to happen this time. I told him I'd never forgive him if he did that again. And I know you needed the money, so all is forgiven."

Adams talks to Eddy. "Tell her to give you the guestimate."

"Did you poison Leslie?" Eddy asks.

"Nah, I didn't have to. We were just drinking. Leslie drinks a lot. I just gave her a shove, and over she went," Wendy says nonchalantly.

"What about Pamala?" Eddy asks, trying to hide his anger.

"The rope thing was an accident. Pamala was just supposed to fall in the water and drown. I don't know how that happened," she says.

"Don't you feel bad at all? These are people's lives. How can you? Why—?"

Adams interrupts. "Calm down, Eddy. You're doing okay."

Eddy closes his eyes and then starts again, "So what's your guestimate?"

"At least twelve. Maybe sixteen. I've mostly killed for you, Eddy. For us," she says.

Eddy stands violently. "There is *no us*! I loved how Littia took care of our son. I loved Kathleen. I was just waiting for your daddy to pay me off again. You make me sick. You are evil."

Wendy is bawling. "No. You love me," she says.

The officer comes over. "Sir, you need to leave," he says sternly.

"Gladly," Eddy says and starts walking. He turns back. "I don't love you. I have never loved you. And I will never love you," he says empathically.

"I'll get you, Eddy! You'll see," Wendy shouts.

Garner turns to Adams, "So, how do you think that went?"

"Ugh… Is that search warrant still in effect?" Adams asks.

Chapter Thirty-Two

THE GOOD, THE BAD, AND THE EVIL

Gretchen is getting antsy. She feels better and wants to do something, anything that is not in the hospital. They have cleared her for outpatient therapy, and Gretchen will be leaving tomorrow. She cannot wait. Being in the sunshine and fresh air will be excellent. Lloyd and Hamer have left. Only Chad is with her.

"So, you'll be going home tomorrow," Chad says with some reservation.

"Yes. I'll be glad and sad. Glad I'm getting better but sad I won't get to see my friends as much," Gretchen says quietly.

Chad is somber. "Thank you for solving Kathleen's murder. It has been good to know the truth. Not just about the murder but about everything. I always felt and thought something wasn't quite right in our marriage. Now I know."

"I'm so sorry. I know that must hurt so much," Gretchen says.

Chad smiles somewhat and looks down at the floor.

Gretchen's heart aches for him. "When my marriage fell apart, I was so sad. My Gramma had left me several letters when she died. On the outside of the envelope, one said, 'If you ever have a marriage that ends in divorce!' It helped me enormously. She explained some things to me that I would never have thought of by myself. She told me I hadn't lost a thing and that my husband, in reality, was a jerk. She said what I was mourning was a figment of my imagination. I was mourning a guy I had created in my mind. I had given him lots of attributes that just didn't exist. She said people do it all the time, especially women but men also do it. Then, when things don't work out, they suffer needlessly. Thinking they've had this tremendous loss. But, in reality, if they saw that person for who they indeed are, they would never have wanted to be with them in the first place.

"Gramma told me to write down on paper an accurate description of my husband and then take a good, hard look at each item listed there. Were they genuinely authentic? If I were honest with myself, I would see I had given him attributes that never existed. I would also see I hadn't lost a thing worth keeping. She was right. She even had me redo the first list I made and had me question everything I put again. She was right about that too. You have to write it down. It's harder to lie to yourself when it's staring back at you on the paper.

"You want to be factual, not emotional, to get to the truth. And to the healing. Gramma saved me a lot of suffering. It still hurt but not nearly as much as it would have. She said she wrote that letter because of my experiences with my mother. She figured I'd need it one day. She was right again. I miss her."

"I think I would've liked your Gramma," Chad says with a smile.

"I know you would have. Truthfully, she had written me about making the attribute list in the letter titled, 'If you think you're in love.' But I ignored it. Should've listened."

"We all make mistakes. Part of life," Chad says kindly.

"Chad, thank you so much for all you've done. You've been such a help and comfort. But you still never told me why you have two identical pools," Gretchen says with a curious look.

"Well, you are going to have to come to visit to find out," he says.

"Will you tell me something else? Why did you stop holding my hand? I've been trying to figure it out," she says. "It was so comforting."

"I didn't realize you knew I was. You were hurt, and you were healing. When you became alert, I didn't want to take advantage of you in your vulnerable state," he says with pure honesty.

"It was nice when you held my hand. I loved it. It was so comforting," Gretchen confesses.

"Then I wish I hadn't stopped," he says, taking her hand and kissing it.

Chad strokes Gretchen's cheek softly with his fingertips. Touching, talking, it feels unbelievable to Gretchen. He gently presses his lips to hers.

Gretchen can hardly breathe. She has never experienced such tenderness, and her heart melts inside her chest. He gently kisses her again.

Placing his hand on the side of Gretchen's face, Chad looks into her eyes. He runs his finger slowly along the outline of her lips. A longing deep inside churns within her. A desire Gretchen almost does not recognize.

Passion engulfs Gretchen as she has never before felt. Chad kisses her again. Gretchen thinks she will explode with feeling. How can this man make her feel like this with just his kiss? Gretchen realizes he is not kissing her with just his lips; he is kissing her with his soul, as well.

All too soon for Gretchen, the kissing stops. Chad strokes her cheek again.

"May I hold you?" he asks.

"Please," she replies, somewhat in shock.

Chad lies in her hospital bed with her and wraps his arms around her. Gretchen places the sheet over Chad. "Please don't ever let go," she says and cuddles into his caress. It is the best night's sleep either one of them has had in a long time, if not ever.

As the morning staff shift changes, the nurse comes into the room and writes on the whiteboard. Chad quietly and quickly slips out of the bed and into the chair.

"Time for vitals, breakfast, and one last physical therapy session before you get to leave this place," she says and turns to see Chad. She squeals. "Who are you?"

"I'm sorry. I'm out of here, going to the cafeteria," Chad says, kissing Gretchen on the top of her head, as he always does when he leaves.

Gretchen hates for him to go. She can't remember ever feeling so happy.

Chad peeks his head back into the room. "I'll be here wait-ing after your physical therapy to drive you home," he says with a big smile and leaves.

~~~

The district attorney calls Adams and Garner to come to his office. He is awaiting their arrival.

"Thanks for coming, fellows. Have a seat," the DA says.

Garner puts a wooden jewelry box with plastic, colorful jewels stuck to the top on the desk.

"This is from Monroe's house, like she said on the tape with Osborne. The search warrant ended at midnight. We got there at ten-thirty p.m. We looked for some kind of a list or info to go with it but didn't find any within the limited time we had," Garner says.

"Thanks for doing that, but we have a bigger problem. I stalled as long as I could, and I think this is a mistake. However, the D.C. prison system has let Wendy Monroe out on bail. The judge set bail at five million, but she easily made that. I gave him a list of serious concerns, but he says she has to have her day in court before she is 'guilty.'

"Take a deep breath. Wendy's attorney claims that all the stuff she told Osborne was to try to impress him. She was try-ing to seem more interesting. Monroe claims she never shoved Leslie or pushed Pamala. Technically, Littia died of a drug and alcohol combination overdose with just Littia's fingerprints all over both bottles and the note," the DA says and takes a drink of water. "They haven't said this yet, but if the snake bite comes up, I'm sure she'll blame Osborne and claim he wanted custody of his son."

"This is nuts! What about all that creepy, poisonous stuff at her house and Gretchen Crandall?" Garner asks in complete frustration.

The DA shakes his head. "Some of the creatures in her house are not even supposed to be in this country. But that boils down to fines—some quite hefty, but just fines. With her bankroll, she won't even notice. Had she been abusing or mistreating them, that could have landed her some jail time. But, according to the experts, they were well cared for in many ways. And I wouldn't be surprised if her father claims all the creatures are his, to protect her."

"But Crandall! That's evidence," Adams says, clenching his teeth.

"You would think. But it falls into the 'he said—she said' category, and with Crandall's physical problems, we need more. Plus, Monroe claims that it was Osborne who tried to kill Crandall. And Osborne was there and attacked Crandall. That plays right into her game. Also, she claims it was Osborne who put the poison in the cup," he says, throwing his hands in the air.

"Wait," Garner exclaims. "The attack at the hospital. Osborne was nowhere around."

"Yes, but technically, that was an attempted attack. It will not get Monroe anywhere near the jail time she deserves. Particularly since this is the first offense. Welcome to my job. Knowing things and proving them are completely different. I am hoping that you guys can come up with more evidence. *Please*," the DA pleads.

"What about Kathleen Fitzgerald?" Adams asks.

The DA huffs. "Working on it. Right now, the only thing for certain I can prove is that Osborne didn't do it. He was in Italy. I haven't been able to put Monroe anywhere near Kathleen Fitzgerald, though. I'm hoping you guys can help me out. With anything!" he says. "That also brings us to another problem. With Monroe out, we have to be concerned about Crandall. I don't trust Monroe. Plan on posting a guard outside Crandall's hospital room. I'm sure the D.C. Police will be happy to help. Please make sure they're on the lookout for a sweet-looking sheep that's an evil villain underneath. Someone they'd never suspect."

"But Crandall's going home. They're moving her to outpatient therapy," Garner says, with a deep exhale.

"Oh, great," the DA says sarcastically. "Just what we need. Well, let Crandall know and tell her to tell all her close friends, so, hopefully, they can help too."

"Do we warn Eddy Osborne that Monroe's out?" Adams asks.

The DA rubs his chin. "I'd just like to let the two of them have at each other. In our line of work, we meet those that have just had some rough breaks, those that are bad, those that are rotten, and those that are downright evil. If you don't believe in evil when you get into this profession, you eventually will. Both of them are in that last category. But we must follow the law, so we need to inform Osborne, especially since Monroe threatened him at the jail.

"Also, I'm issuing two restraining orders for the maximum distance to keep Monroe legally away from Crandall and Osborne. However, we all know that restraining orders don't stop bullets or attacks. They only work for law-abiding citizens and usually end up as evidence in prosecutions. But we need to do everything we can. With any luck, we can catch her violating the order—anything to buy time," the DA says.

Chapter Thirty-Three

BEWARE OF BLUNDERS

Gretchen finishes her physical therapy at the hospital. Then she is immediately discharged, and Chad is driving her to her apartment.

Chad looks at Gretchen as he drives. "How does it feel to finally be out of the hospital? Nineteen days is a long time."

"It feels wonderful. A little scary but great," Gretchen replies.

"Well, some things have transpired, and we need to make a change to our plans," Chad says.

"What's up?" she asks.

"You need to pack your bags. You are coming to stay with us at Hamer's. His house is big and will work well. Unless, of course, you want us all to come here," he laughs, trying to lighten the mood. "Wendy is out on bail, and the police were planning to station an officer outside your hospital room. That's how serious they think things are."

"Oh dear," Gretchen says.

"It will be fine. I don't even think Wendy could know about Hamer. And even if she does, we've got things covered," Chad says, trying to be as reassuring as possible. "Pack everything you think you'll need for a while because the detectives don't want you to make any trips back here. They believe this is the most likely place she'll be looking to find you or follow you. Here or at your physical therapy. But we've taken care of that.

"We've rented some equipment from Virginia that's coming to Hamer's. Also, we've hired a physical therapist in Virginia who will be driving an hour to come to his house, too. In addition, I've hired four personal armed bodyguards to protect you at all times. Just in case. I wish I had known Wendy was getting out of jail; I would've had her followed 24/7. So far, they can't find her. They're trying. But we have the guards because you can never be too careful. So, no worries. Okay? Just continue to get better," Chad says and hugs Gretchen tightly at the red light.

"Oh, thank you so much," Gretchen sighs. "I wouldn't have had a clue what to do. I'm still reeling, and to be honest, Wendy is a homicidal maniac, and she terrifies me."

"At this point, Wendy terrifies us all!" Chad replies.

~~~

Eddy is still out on bail. He is waiting for his next photography assignment and enjoying the gorgeous day on his veranda. The phone rings, breaking the silence. He does not recognize the number, but he answers. "Hello."

"Hi, Eddy. It's me," Wendy says.

Eddy starts to hang up but decides to hear what she will say, thinking she is still in jail.

"What?" he says harshly.

"I want you to know that those things you said to me at the jail hurt a lot. I couldn't believe you could be so mean! The two times you broke up with me before, you weren't mean about it. You said you were sorry it hadn't worked out. I thought you had met someone else. But both times I found out that you weren't with somebody new. You went to visit your mother. Of course, I didn't know that Daddy had paid you to go away because he didn't think you were good enough for me. Or our family. I thought it was adorable that you had gone to see your mom the first time. Not so much the second time. I—"

Eddy interrupts, demanding, "How do you know I went to see Momma?"

"Oh, that doesn't matter now," she says. "I'm sending you something. I hope you enjoy it. Talk to you soon."

Wendy hangs up, which has never happened before. Eddy always has had to hang up first. It seems a little curious to him, but he just hopes she has finally gotten the message that he is not interested in her whatsoever.

There is a knock at Eddy's door. When he answers, he is surprised to see Garner and Adams.

They are there to inform him of Wendy's release and that the district attorney has issued a restraining order on her since she threatened him at the jail.

"I'm not afraid of that little cockroach. I hope she tries something. I'll finish whatever she starts," Eddy says defiantly.

"Well, be alert," Adams warns. "She uses deadly spiders and snakes and poisons. It's unlikely you'll see her, just her evil handiwork. Here's a card with both of our direct cell numbers.

Call us anytime if you see or hear anything, and don't hesitate to call 911 no matter what it is."

"She just called me a few minutes ago, from a number I've never seen. She said she's sending me something," Eddy tells them.

"Give us that number. And do not touch anything Monroe sends you. The box or the envelope could be tainted or laced with some poison. Call us immediately. And remember, what she's sending may not come to your mailbox or door. It might slither or creep in through some unseen hole or crack. You cannot be too careful," Garner says.

About an hour after the detectives leave Eddy's house, there is another knock at the door. Eddy looks out of the peephole and sees a courier his agency often uses with an envelope. He opens the door and starts to take the package.

Eddy hesitates. "Ah, just put it on the step. Leave it there."

"Huh?" the courier responds.

"Just leave it on the step! I'll get it later," Eddy says harshly.

The courier does as directed and leaves without a tip. Eddy calls the detectives. They have the hazardous material team inspect the package. There is nothing dangerous anywhere. Also, no fingerprints belonging to Wendy are on any of it. There are just photographs in an envelope. Garner and Adams bring the material back to Eddy. He places the package on the table and returns to what he was doing.

Eddy is caulking his computer room as extensively as possible. It is the only room he has without windows. It is on the third floor and has a skylight. He has moved a bed and television in there and plans to consider it his safe room. He has even caulked every outlet twice to be extra cautious. Eddy is wearing boots, jeans, and a leather jacket to make any biting harder to do.

Feeling rather accomplished, Eddy goes to get some food to bring upstairs. He added wood to the bottom of the door to seal it, and he must push hard against the carpet to even get out of the room. "Safety achieved," he says. "That wench is *not* getting me."

Eddy makes a sandwich. He packs his cooler with drinks and dips for his chips. Watching a good movie to take his mind off things will help him relax, Eddy plans. On his way back upstairs, he grabs the package off the table. Eddy finishes his sandwich and picks out his movie. Then he opens the envelope and looks at the pictures.

Eddy screams and wails, falling to his knees. He cries until dawn!

Chapter Thirty-Four

FACING THE TRUTH IS NOT ALWAYS EASY

Eddy forces himself up off the floor as the sun comes through the skylight. He has been awake all night and crying until his eyes are almost swollen shut. Eddy waits until seven a.m. and then calls Adams to come to his house.

When Garner and Adams arrive and enter, they cannot believe how bad Eddy looks.

"Man, what happened to you?" Adams asks.

Eddy looks at them. "Worse than snakes, or spiders, or poison!" he says and throws the pictures on the table. "Those are pictures of my momma I've never seen. In the last two, she's dead. Wendy must have killed her! My momma had a heart attack, and now I know why. Wendy killed my momma. And it's all my fault. And Kathleen and Littia. But Momma? She was good and honest and loving. The closest thing to a saint you'd ever meet. Wendy killed my momma." Eddy starts crying again.

"Eddy, we're so sorry," Garner says.

"It's not your fault, Eddy. Wendy did this, *not* you," Adams says.

Eddy appreciates the words, but his emotions run deep. He wipes the tears from his face. "Yeah, but I brought her into their lives. What did you find out about the phone number?"

"It's a burn phone. Already thrown away with no evidence. We were afraid of that, but we're still going to get Monroe," Adams says adamantly.

"How? The phone won't work. We already know that there's no fingerprint evidence on the package or the pictures. I'll sign a permit to exhume my momma's body, but somehow she keeps getting away with everything," Eddy says in frustration.

"She has been clever. But they always slip up. They get cocky and forget something. It will happen, and when it does, we'll get her." Adams says.

Garner adds, "He's right. We'll get her. We thought we had her with the courier. She hired a teenage boy to deliver the envelope, and he hired another teenage boy. They both still had the money they received, but no luck. There were no prints or chemicals. We knew the money paid to the courier would be clean, but we hope we'll get her on the back end. The third teenage boy that we think is the initial contact is missing."

"You're not getting her soon enough! She keeps killing," Eddy says with his signature snarl.

~~~

Everyone is on high alert for the next three weeks, but things are quiet. No one hears from Wendy. Hamer goes on various assignments and emails his material through the police department, avoiding physical contact with the newspaper office. Hamer texts Phyllis updates on Gretchen through burn phones that the police provided, but Chad funded. Phyllis keeps everyone informed but never mentions where Gretchen is staying. Most of the staff think she has retreated to Chad's private island.

Lloyd and Phyllis stroll down the street to a park bench and are there for a long while. The entire time they are gone, the staff speculates on what is happening. When they return, Phyllis announces that she will take some vacation time to see her sick aunt in Pennsylvania.

Gretchen and Chad spend lots of time together, but they are never alone. Chad wishes he had a gun permit for here, but he does not. They have reached the point of having some pretty private conversations and ignoring the armed guards.

"You keep worrying about me not having had enough time to grieve, but I've had more time than you realize," Chad admits. "I grieved at the hospital and hotel when I wasn't in the room with you. And, truthfully, I grieved a lot on the island by myself for years. A lot. Yes, I didn't know everything, but I knew things weren't right with us. And I knew Kathleen's life choices more than likely had gotten her killed. I spent years trying to figure things out. Before that, I spent years hoping things would get better. They never did, only worse. However, I had no idea how worse! In many ways, finding out the awful facts has been a real relief. Sometimes, the truth does set you free." Chad hopes Gretchen will believe him.

Gretchen starts to say something, but Chad begins again. "And what was it your Gramma said about loving a figment of your imagination? That makes a lot of sense to me. I think I was doing that the whole time I was with Kathleen. Because if I had known who she was and what she was doing, I would never have wanted to be with her. I guess that's why she went to such lengths to hide her true identity. So, no more talk of grieving. I think I should be celebrating. Not to sound cold. Just being honest."

Not knowing what to say, to Chad's surprise, Gretchen gives him a big kiss and a huge hug. "Hamer will be here soon. Let's make everybody 'celebration' banana splits with different ice creams, lots of chocolate syrup, pecans, organic dark cherries, and homemade whip cream. We'll have celebration banana splits for dinner. How does that sound?" she asks.

"Wonderful," Chad responds. He then takes Gretchen's face in his hands and passionately kisses her for a long time. At this point, the guard blushes and turns away quietly.

~~~

Adams and Garner are in their unmarked car. "Why can't we find this woman?" Adams asks. "She's up to something. Things have been way too quiet. It's been over three weeks and not a peep. That has me very nervous and uncomfortable."

"Me too," Garner agrees. "But the DA says she's out on bail, and without something new happening, we have no grounds to track her. She'll turn up. We just have to be patient."

"Well, my nightmares are on overdrive. Not knowing makes it worse. Her evil is way beyond my imagination!" Adams confesses.

~~~

Eddy sits in the dark in his living room, still beating himself up over his mother's death. He has been drinking quite heavily and does not know what to do with himself. Nothing matters to him anymore. Part of him wishes Wendy *would* send something deadly his way. He would prefer that to the slow torture he is enduring.

The phone rings. It is again a number Eddy has never seen. He answers. A young child's voice is on the other end.

"Mr. Eddy, my name is Winston. You don't know me, but my new nanny knows you…"

Eddy goes into a complete panic and sobers up immediately! Winston is his son with Littia. He does not know Eddy, and Eddy does not know him. They had agreed that Littia's husband, a very good man, would be Winston's only dad. That is especially important since Littia and her husband have other children. This way, Winston would have a better and more normal life. Eddy has no idea why or how he would be calling him but feels it cannot be good. Also, the phrase "my new nanny" has Eddy petrified.

"I'm gonna be four years old in two months. Do you want to come to my birthday party?" Winston asks.

"Winston, hi, buddy. How are you? Where are you?" Eddy asks.

"We're in the car," the boy answers. "We're going to the amusement park. It's going to be so much fun. And I get to watch a movie on the way there."

"Who all is in the car with you?" Eddy asks.

"Oh, just me and Wendy. She's taking me on a special trip; my brothers and sisters have school," he says.

"Are you driving right now, or are you stopped?" Eddy asks.

"We stopped to go to the bathroom and call you," he replies.

"It's been nice talking to you, Winston. You are a smart boy. Can I please talk to Wendy now?" Eddy says, trying to hide his panic and fear.

"Sure," Winston says and hands the phone to Wendy. "He wants to talk to you."

Wendy sets the phone down, but Eddy can hear. "Let's get your headphones back on and get your movie playing again. You eat your fries and enjoy your show," she says, picking the phone back up and talking to Eddy.

"Did you think I forgot you? That's never going to happen," she says with a sinister laugh.

"Wendy, where are you? What are you doing?"

"Wouldn't you like to know? That's not going to happen either," she says.

"Listen to me, Wendy. We've got to talk. I've had a lot of time to think, and I was so wrong. I am so sorry I hurt you. That was not right at all—"

"You got that right!" she interrupts.

"Wendy, listen. I never meant those things I said at the jail. It's you I love and want to be with always. I love you. And only you. Just you," Eddy says in desperation.

"Why should I believe you? You're just trying to trick me because I've got Winston."

"No, I want to be with you right now and forever. Tell me where you are, and I'll come there. I'll leave this minute. I want to see you so much. Do you know why Winston is my son's name? Because Wendy starts with W. Wendy and Winston."

"W for real? How do I know you won't just send the police?"

"I tell you what. Do you remember your parents' secluded cabin in the Blue Ridge Mountains? Let's meet there right now, as soon as we can get there. We can spend the next month there planning our life together and everything we want to do. How many kids we'll have, and where we want to live. I want to hold you and kiss you and tell you how much I love you. I want to make up for all the pain I've caused you. Will you meet me there?" Eddy asks in his most charming way.

"I was right; you do love me!" Wendy says with total enthusiasm. "Yes, I'll meet you there. I'm closer than you are, so I'll stop and get some groceries and supplies. Hurry, hurry as fast as you can, Eddy."

"If you get there first, which you probably will, read Winston a bedtime story and sing him some songs. I want to see what a good mom you're going to be. I'm so excited to see you," he says, hoping Winston will still be alive when he arrives.

"Okay. I love you, Eddy! I'll see you soon," she says.

"I love you, too, Wendy. Drive safe. Bye," he says.

That ruse was the only thing Eddy could think of to do. He knows that Wendy has taken Winston to kill him and further hurt and punish Eddy. He has been thinking nonstop these last three weeks. Eddy does feel bad for using Wendy for her money and her status. He now knows that was wrong, and much of everything else in his life has been wrong—everything except the love he has for his mother. However, Eddy failed her. He failed Kathleen. He failed Littia. Not to mention a whole host of other women he hurt and damaged tremendously along the way. He cannot fail Winston. That is the only good thing he has left. The only thing of value for all the years he has been alive. He has to save Winston.

There is no time to contact Adams and Garner. Plus, he is afraid they may mess up something. He knows they are well-meaning, but they have not been successful so far. He cannot take any chances. Winston's life is literally at stake!

As Eddy is driving to the cabin, he comes to a dramatic realization. He got so caught up in the high society lifestyle that it never dawned on him that he put himself in an impossible situation. Eddy truly was looking for a good woman, like his mother. Yet, he wanted a high society wife. So, he was looking for a good woman in a pool of females that usually does not spawn the kind of good woman he wants. One who works hard to take care of her children, loving them totally and wanting to be with them and raise them. Certainly not farming them out to some boarding school or handing them over to a nanny.

Eddy's two goals were at cross purposes. The only good woman he had met was Gretchen, and she was not high society enough for him. He now feels that not only is he a complete and utter failure but a total imbecile. So many of the people he admired and longed to be with were just self-centered, self-serving, pathetic excuses for human beings. They only ever did good things for other people to see them doing good, not that they ever really cared. All the schmoozing, all the parties, all the banquets, all the nonsense, was a waste of time. Ultimately, it was a complete and utter waste of his life. Saving Winston is a must!

Chapter Thirty-Five

CHANCES AND CHOICES

Eddy reaches the cabin in record time, under three hours. He is glad he did not get stopped for speeding because he certainly was. Eddy always implements the advice a cab driver friend taught him. Never be the fastest car and do not drive in the fast lane—just use it to pass. That information has served him well. It took Eddy some time to get certain things together he brought with him. It is almost midnight.

Wendy's car is there, and the lights are on inside the house. Eddy is hoping desperately that he finds Winston unharmed. He has gone through half of a bottle of Tums on the drive there. Touching the front doorknob, he breaks out in a cold sweat, fearing what he will see.

To his surprise, Wendy has started a fire and is sitting in the rocking chair holding Winston. The child looks as if he is sleeping peacefully. Eddy hopes that is what has happened and that he is not dead. Eddy caresses Wendy's head and hugs her.

"I tried to keep him awake, but he just conked out. I sang him three songs; he seemed to like them," Wendy says, looking lovingly at Eddy.

"Nice job. You look so sweet together. I can carry Winston to bed."

Eddy takes Winston as Wendy smiles. Eddy purposely jostles Winston to see if he will move and is okay. Winston does stir like a sleeping child, to Eddy's relief. Wendy and Eddy tuck Winston in bed together. They each kiss him goodnight.

Wendy has on an elegant dark lavender nightgown and robe. She thinks that is a good color for her pale skin. Eddy takes her hand as they walk down the steps.

"You look beautiful. That's a pretty set on you," Eddy says, trying to be charming to buy time to think. When they reach the bottom of the stairs, he takes Wendy in his arms and kisses her. He is struggling because he cannot forget that she killed his mother.

"It feels so right to be in your arms again. I love you so much, Eddy! I'm glad we are back together. Where we belong, never again to be apart," Wendy says, with much affection.

Eddy has debated many different scenarios contemplating how he could be with Wendy. How could he get past knowing what she has done, especially killing his mother? Even if Eddy was only with her as penance for his past wrongs. However, he knows he will make a mistake at some point that will make Wendy mad, which would again put Winston's life in danger. Currently, he is just making a plan as he goes and deciding what to do moment by moment.

"I brought some excellent wine for this special occasion. It's new and all the rage in Paris," he says and goes to the car.

Eddy gets two bottles of wine, one for each of them, and a bottle of scotch from the car. When he returns, Wendy has taken off her robe. She is sitting on the cozy rug in front of the fire. She points to her scarred arm.

"Remember how much I love you?" Wendy asks.

"I do," he says, popping the cork and handing Wendy a fancy bottle wrapped in a linen cloth.

"This is a contest. Now, it's an acquired taste, so we have to get used to it. Lots of fun things are going to happen. And some games to celebrate," Eddy says. "First a shot of scotch," he says, handing Wendy her shot glass and guzzling his. She drinks hers.

"Now, the wine. Take as much as you can drink at one time. Even if you have to hold your nose because you don't like the taste," Eddy says, holding his nose and drinking as much as he can.

"Yuck. That's nasty," Eddy says. "But the good part's coming."

Wendy has trouble drinking it but forces herself so that she will be going along with the game. They take another shot of scotch and then more wine. As the bottles start to empty, Eddy picks up Wendy and says, "Now for some games." He carries her into the bedroom with a bed made with metal rails creating a sleigh bed. He places her on the bed and has her drink more of her wine. She hates the taste but holds her nose to help.

"Here comes the fun," he says, handing her a pouch of handcuffs. "Take out one of the handcuffs and cuff your left foot to one of the fat bottom rails. Pull it tight, so there's no escape. Good job. Now take out the key and throw it across the room. Okay. Do the same with your right foot. Spread your foot over. Pull it tight and throw the key. Wine time—drink up. Hold your nose. You're doing fine."

Even though Wendy hates the wine, she loves all of this attention from Eddy. He has never done any surprises or games like this with her before tonight. She finishes her bottle.

"My stomach hurts; it's so full," Wendy says.

"Here, have some Tums. They do wonders," he says, pouring some on the bed for Wendy.

She takes two and almost misses her mouth because she is quite woozy.

Eddy hands Wendy the pouch again. "One more time," he says. "Cuff your left hand to the top rail. You may have to hook two cuffs together to get them to reach. You know the drill." She does as Eddy instructs and then throws the key as far as possible. By this time, her head is spinning.

"No, no, no. Don't pass out yet. You have to hear the most important part. I tried everything to figure out how we could be together. But there's no way it works with Winston being safe. I would always have to worry about you killing him to hurt me or because I cared more about him than you. That just can't happen. He deserves a life—a nice life. So, what's happening is, for all the people you've killed or destroyed in some fashion—especially my momma—you are going to lie here and die a long and agonizing death. Painful, too. That's what antifreeze laced with wine does. I had cranberry juice. No one will hear you in this secluded area. And you said your mom and dad extended their trip at least another two weeks so they won't be missing you. This way, you will never kill anyone or hurt anyone again. And most importantly, Winston will be safe!"

Wendy tries to speak. "You can't..."

Eddy starts to leave and turns back as Wendy makes weak attempts to pull herself free. "For what it's worth, I am sorry I hurt you. And if I get caught and go to jail or worse, it's worth it. So, Winston can be safe and free from your wicked plans! By the way, Winston was Littia's maiden name." Wendy passes out and goes completely limp.

After cleaning up and placing the pouch in the car, Eddy leaves Wendy's bottle with just her prints. He only touched it with the cloth. Eddy gingerly picks up Winston. He places him in the backseat of his car, snuggling him tightly with his blanket and pillow from his house.

Eddy drives the speed limit. They make it back while it is still dark. Eddy places Winston on the bench close to Winston's neighborhood community hospital, still asleep. No surveillance cameras reach that far. He hopes they think Wendy had a change of heart. Winston never saw Eddy; he slept the whole time. However, Eddy is thrilled he got to see Winston. He can't believe how much he loves him. Eddy's encounter with Winston is causing him to rethink even more of the things in his life.

~~~

Gretchen has fallen asleep on the couch after her physical therapy. Chad is starting dinner. The doorbell rings. The bodyguard rushes to the door. He looks to see who it is.

"It's not Wendy," the guard says.

Chad joins him and looks. "It's Phyllis," he says, quite surprised, as he opens the door.

Gretchen is awake now and comes into the room.

Phyllis steps into the foyer. "Now, before you guys go getting your feathers all ruffled," she says, "I want you to know that I drove to Pennsylvania to visit my aunt first, so I could drive here without being followed. I even rented a car just in case someone has put a tracker on mine. I watch television, too, you know. You guys said we couldn't be too careful."

"Well, good thinking there, Phyllis," Chad says. "It's nice to see you."

Gretchen hugs Phyllis. "Is anything wrong?"

"Nothing's wrong. I just need to talk to you," Phyllis says. "Alone!"

"Well, that doesn't exactly happen around here," Gretchen replies, shrugging her shoulders.

"Where's the biggest bathroom?" Phyllis asks.

Gretchen points the way, thinking Phyllis needs to go. Phyllis grabs Gretchen's arm.

"You're coming with me for some girl talk. I doubt they'll follow us in there," Phyllis says, giggling. Gretchen smiles and follows her.

Once they reach the bathroom, Phyllis closes the door and gives Gretchen a huge hug. "I miss you," she says.

Gretchen hugs her back. "I miss you, too," she replies.

Phyllis closes the toilet lid and sits down, motioning for Gretchen to sit on the side of the bathtub.

"I can't stop thinking about everything. I sure wish your Gramma had told you this, but I'm going to since she didn't. Chad Fitzgerald is very much in love with you. And you're in love with him. On top of that, he needs you. It's written all over his face. You're the best thing that's ever happened to him. And he's the best thing that's ever happened to you. Both of you need to stop this pussyfooting around and get married. You can come back to the newsroom once a month to see us, especially so Lloyd won't freak out. But you need to get this show on the road. Particularly if your Gramma's right and you're having three kids. You need to get started!" Phyllis says, hardly stopping to breathe.

"Well, um…" Gretchen says, and Phyllis interrupts.

"That brings me to another point. I keep trying to tell myself that you imagined seeing your Gramma. But I can't ignore you seeing me sitting with Lloyd! That's driving me nuts. So, if you have three kids, I want you to promise me you'll try everything to have number four. Because your Gramma only said three. And we'll see what happens and take it from there. Do you have any good news for me?"

"Yes. With everything that's happened, I've lost fifteen pounds," Gretchen says excitedly.

"What? I'm saying all this, and that's what you come up with? No, girlfriend. Has Chad asked you to marry him?"

Gretchen is flabbergasted. She is not sure what to say. "Ahh, nooo," she replies hesitantly.

"Well, you're out," Phyllis motions. "And Chad's in," Phyllis says emphatically.

"You…you…you can't," Gretchen stammers.

"Look, you know I love you to bits. But I've been driving for two days to make it here to say my piece. And say it, I will, or snap. Please," Phyllis says adamantly.

"But I think he's afraid of marriage and of trusting. Look what he's been through! You can't push him," Gretchen pleads.

"If he's going to namby-pamby his way through this garbage, he's going to lose a big chunk of his life," Phyllis says sternly. "All the more reason he needs a wake-up call or a swift kick. If he needs reassurances that you're nothing like Kathleen, I'm the person to give those to him. He is not going to know what I've said to you. That's confidential. And you're not going to know what I say to him. It boils down to three things, and you know these. One—I don't play games. Never have. Never will. I'm a straight shooter, as they say. Two—I hate to see people I care about stuck in a game they don't even recognize. What a waste of precious time and valuable life. Three—If I didn't care, I wouldn't be here. So, go get me Chad, please."

After that genuine and passionate outpouring, Gretchen cannot think of anything to say. She dutifully goes to get Chad.

"She wants me to go where?" Chad says with a grin.

"Trust me. Just go, or Phyllis will be out here. Please," Gretchen says sweetly.

Chad smiles and walks to the bathroom. Gretchen is a bit apprehensive as she stands in the living room watching him close the door. Chad sits on the side of the bathtub, looking at Phyllis the whole time.

"Thank you, Chad. So, when do you plan on asking Gretchen to marry you?"

Chad is stunned and speechless. He just sits there, not knowing what to say.

"You are in love with her, aren't you?" Phyllis asks matter-of-factly.

"Ah, is it that obvious?" he asks.

"No. I'm just incredibly observant." She laughs, and Chad laughs too, welcoming the relief.

"I know I can be pretty straightforward, but I hate to see those I care about waste time, especially at your age," Phyllis says, not meaning to voice the last phrase.

"Whew! Well, I plan on asking her to marry me when I think she'll say yes, and I have a ring," Chad admits.

"Are you afraid Gretchen could end up being like Kathleen? Or afraid of marriage?" she asks.

"Not at all. Gretchen is nothing like Kathleen. And marriage should be wonderful. I was just with the wrong person," Chad says.

"So, it's not your fear of marriage or commitment; it's your fear of rejection! And needing the security of a ring," Phyllis states.

"Well, I never thought of it like that," he says.

"You love her. She loves you. Bite the bullet and go ahead and ask her. You can look for a ring together online. Time to get married and get working on those babies," Phyllis says with a huge smile. "Who knows how long that lunatic Wendy will cause you guys to need to be in hiding."

Chapter Thirty-Six

FREEDOM

It is late afternoon before Eddy rises. After having not slept for weeks, he enjoys sleeping quite soundly for the first time since the whole fiasco with Wendy got terrible. There is a knock on the door. Eddy is no longer afraid to answer. It is Adams and Garner.

"Hi, Eddy," Adams says. "Can we come in?"

Eddy invites them in and gets everyone a cup of coffee. They sit at the kitchen table.

Adam starts. "We kind of found out what Wendy has been up to and want to warn you to be on high alert. Early this morning, your son, Winston, was found outside the community hospital close to where he lives. Everything's alright, and he's unharmed. But Wendy got a job as a nanny for Littia's children. With her sweetness routine, that wouldn't be hard at all. We never thought to warn Littia's husband about her.

"She was supposed to be taking Winston to King's Dominion for a memorable trip. All the other kids are older and in school. They were supposed to be gone for two days. But then Winston ended up back here, just dropped off at the hospital. No Wendy. We think maybe she was going to hurt him or snatch him but had a change of heart. That's all we can figure. Winston says they never made it to the amusement park. But he remembers talking to a guy named Eddy on the phone but never saw him. Did you hear anything from Wendy or Winston?"

"No. You know that Winston doesn't know I'm his father, right? That was the agreement, and it remains in effect. Winston's dad must be furious after all Wendy's done. Are you ever going to get her in prison where she belongs?" Eddy asks, trying to remain calm. He is thankful Winston is safe.

"We hope," Garner says. "It's a strange occurrence, but maybe that little fellow got to her. He's mighty cute. But you watch out and let us know if you hear anything. We're still just a phone call away."

Eddy is surprised he was not afraid when the detectives came. He kept thinking they might arrest him. Eddy tries to convince himself that he is prepared for whatever happens. As Detective Garner said, Winston is "mighty cute," and Eddy is relieved that he is back home, unharmed and safe.

~~~

Several days pass quietly. No one has discussed Phyllis's visit. Gretchen's health is improving, and she is coming along well. Her walking is almost back to normal. However, she still struggles with the stairs. Being cooped up, they are all getting a bit stir crazy. Chad wishes they could sit on the deck or in the yard, but the safest place is in the house.

Chad has Hamer pick up a delicious dinner from a fancy restaurant downtown. After sharing the excellent meal, Hamer goes to bed, and one guard naps in the chair. Chad and Gretchen are on the couch watching a movie and eating a bowl of popcorn. All of a sudden, Chad pauses the movie and turns to Gretchen.

"They say 'there's no time like the present.'" Chad drops to the floor on one knee. "Gretchen Crandall, you are the most amazing woman I have ever known. I am madly in love with you and want to spend every minute of my life with you. I want us to have children and make a loving home and family." Chad takes Gretchen's face in his hands. "And be together for always and forever. Gretchen, will you please marry me?"

Gretchen is totally surprised. When Phyllis first left, Gretchen hoped something might happen, but it did not. So, she thought Chad was not ready and forgot about it. Now, her heart is melting, the way Chad always seems to be able to do quickly. Happy tears start flowing. "Yes! I would love to marry you! This is the most incredible moment of my life." Also, Chad's as well.

They repeatedly kiss, savoring every second. Then Chad asks, "May I hold you?"

"Please," she responds. "And never let go."

"I can now say I *never* will."

They sleep on the couch all night. When Hamer gets up, he finds them sound asleep and the guard tiptoeing around in the kitchen. Hamer is not as quiet. Chad and Gretchen awake.

"Good morning, Mr. Fitzgerald," Gretchen says, covering her mouth.

"Good morning, Mrs. Fitzgerald soon to be," Chad says. He takes two breath mints from his pocket, placing one in each of their mouths. He knows her well. "I'm going to take good care of you, and I hope to make you happy every day and night. Oh, and afternoons, as well," he says, as Gretchen drinks in the love.

"I have popcorn kernels in my teeth," she says.

Chad reaches into his pocket and pulls out a small disposable toothbrush that comes with a small dab of toothpaste. "Voila," he says with a big smile. "Just like you use for emergencies."

"So, you had this planned?" she asks.

"Well, not so much. I've been carrying these in my pocket for weeks. I'm just trying to impress you. Is it working?" They both laugh.

Chad caresses Gretchen's cheek. "After breakfast, we'll start looking for your ring online, considering the circumstances." They kiss.

Hamer comes in. "Give it a rest already," he says and laughs. "Do I detect love in the air?"

"Yes, and wedding bells!" Gretchen says, smiling from ear to ear.

"Now, I have some real news to text Phyllis," Hamer chuckles. "So, when are you getting hitched?"

"How about next week?" Chad asks. "Unless you want a big wedding? In which case, we'll have to wait until Wendy's in jail."

"Nope. Been there, done that, not all it's cracked up to be. Next week it is! To quote Phyllis, 'The sooner, the better. Being with the right person is much more important than wasting time and money on some fancy venue,'" Gretchen says, and they all chuckle.

They plan a quick and quiet ceremony. Too much work has gone into keeping Gretchen safe, and they do not want to take any chances now. Hamer takes care of the paperwork. He also arranges for his Christian minister to come to the house to perform the ceremony. Hamer is excited he is going to be the best man.

Phyllis *insists* Lloyd and the prayer ladies go to Pennsylvania to see her aunt. Then Phyllis brings them to Hamer's for the wedding, not knowing until ten minutes before they arrive what is happening. It is a big surprise for everyone. Lloyd gives Gretchen away. He cries lots of happy tears.

However, best of all, the beautiful and costly rings they ordered do not make it in time. Chad borrows one of Hamer's mom's rings and temporarily attaches the clear encased mustard seed to it with some white poster putty. The mustard seed stands out even more. Gretchen loves it.

It is an excellent day for everyone, particularly Chad and Gretchen! This is truly the happiest day of both of their lives.

~~~

Wendy's parents return from their trip. They cannot find Wendy, and the house is a wreck from the legal searches. They call the sheriff. The Monroe's emergency service assistance enables the police to locate Wendy's car at their cabin. She is dead inside. Wendy had scratched her arm, legs, and stomach, getting blood to write. She wrote on the sheet, "Eddy killed me!" However, the only fingerprints on the handcuffs, keys, and wine bottle are hers. There is no evidence whatsoever that Eddy has been to the cabin.

Adams and Garner go to Eddy's home once more.

"Man, she tried to get you. She said she was going to. Monroe tried framing you for murder. But she slipped up. They usually do. No evidence. None. Her parents extended their trip. They left her a message at the house. Monroe probably counted on them getting back in time to save her. Then she'd be alive, and you'd be in jail. It looks like Monroe had a pretty horrible death, too. I don't know why she didn't take pills, although they're more painful than people think. Monroe always went for the drama. Anyway, the nightmare is over. You can sleep well tonight," Adams says.

And Eddy did.

~~~

Chad hires six bodyguards to protect the outside of Hamer's house. He rents Hamer a hotel suite. Now, he and Gretchen can have Hamer's home to themselves for their honeymoon since they cannot safely go anywhere.

Gretchen snuggles in Chad's arm. "I love you so much, and I feel so blessed," she says.

"When we can get out again, what would you like to do? Where would you like to go?" he asks.

"I'd like to go spend some time on your island. Just the two of us," Gretchen says.

"That's our island, Mrs. Fitzgerald," Chad says with a chuckle.

She smiles, and he kisses the top of her head.

"I would like for us to have the island to ourselves a big chunk of the year," Gretchen says, smiling. "With our kids, of course. Then I would like to build cabins and have counselors, making a summer camp. Where kids can come for a week or two to learn to swim, fish, build campfires and enjoy nature through the summer months. Oh, and swim with the turtles. And get to do all the things kids don't get to do much anymore.

"And I would like them to see a real loving couple and family, so they can know what's possible. That would be us, you know. We can give all the girls a clear acrylic heart with a mustard seed inside and all the boys a clear arrowhead with a mustard seed. Or we let them pick which one they want. I remember the first time I was at your island thinking it's too wonderful for just one person—or just one family. This way, tons of kids can feel the joy."

"Of course, that's what you'd want to do! You are terrific. No wonder I love you so much. And it's nice knowing I see and love the real you," he says and kisses her passionately.

"Sorry to spoil the moment, but I have to pee." Gretchen laughs and hurries to the bathroom.

"I'm checking the weather," Chad says and turns on the television.

"Wealthy heiress, Wendy Monroe, was found dead in her family's cabin…"

What?" Chad and Gretchen both yell.

"Call Adams and Garner. See if it's her or another trick," Gretchen says frantically.

~~~

Chad and Gretchen helicopter to their island for a real honeymoon the following day. It is terrific to be there and to be free. They walk all over the grounds, kissing about every thirty steps. Finally, they reach the pools.

"Well, you want to know about the pools." Chad grins. He gingerly pushes Gretchen into the first identical pool. She pulls him in with her as she goes. They laugh and kiss. Gretchen shivers.

"It's freezing!" she chatters.

"Come with me," Chad says, taking Gretchen's hand and leading her out of the pool. "I'll warm you up."

Gretchen is still shivering. Chad picks Gretchen up and jumps into the other identical pool.

"Aaawww. It's heated. I should've realized," Gretchen smiles. They laugh.

"This feels wonderful," she says.

"Yes, it does!" Chad holds Gretchen closely. "And I am never letting go. Not ever."

They kiss passionately. Chad claps three times, and lighted fountains flow with choreographed water and music. "We are soooo lucky," Chad says.

"I think you mean blessed. My luck is not this good. And I am soooo thankful," Gretchen adds.

Chad smiles. "You know, Walt Disney and Mickey have always encouraged me to look for the good and reach for the best part of life. Now, I'm holding that in my arms—you."

They kiss passionately again and then playfully start a water fight. Lights come on surrounding all the pools, forming the shape of Mickey Mouse.

Chapter Thirty-Seven

So, Sigh, Eddy

Since Littia is deceased, Eddy receives a letter from her through her attorney.

"If you are reading this, I am dead. I just want you to please leave Winston with my husband. He is the best man I've ever known, and he has always deserved way better than me. He strongly believes that children come into this world innocent and should not be burdened with garbage their parents and other adults put on them. He does everything possible to give them an incredible life. I think it's important for you to know that one of the other four children is not his, as well. The child biologically belongs to a man I had a brief affair with years ago. He knows nothing of the child's existence. As far as I'm concerned, the child belongs to my husband. Although, my husband does know the truth. Like I said, he has always deserved way better than me. I will not tell you to which child I am referencing. It doesn't matter, because he will give all five children the very best life they can have! There should be more selfless people like him in the world."

Eddy had already come to that conclusion on his own. He does want the best for Winston. Eddy has thought a lot lately. In reality, he cannot stop thinking.

Now Eddy is racked with guilt and fear of getting caught. He regrets many, but not all, of his evil actions. Even though he had a traumatic childhood, there is no excuse for what he has done and the pain he has caused. Eddy's choices resulted in his mother's murder, which gravely torments him. The guilt consumes his every moment.

Also, instead of being enamored with the high society life-style, Eddy is now repulsed by it. He feels it is shallow and even sad. He finally recognizes so much wasted time and resources, and he comprehends so many misused lives. Many people pretending to care and doing good deeds only for show. Eddy laments how much of his time he squandered on nonsense. In addition, he is terrified of getting caught for Wendy's murder.

Hourly, Eddy fears getting arrested. He knows he will not do well in prison. Requesting a death sentence may be preferable to what Eddy would endure should he get caught. Carrying so much emotional baggage, he is a complete mess. Eddy thinks if the law doesn't get him, karma will take him out. He expects to drop dead of a heart attack or have a brain aneurysm. At least, Eddy hopes it is that painless, as flashes of Wendy's agonizing death race through his mind. Ultimately, Eddy feels Wendy got what she deserved for killing his mother, but what is it that he warrants for all his evil acts? Constantly, Eddy is a wreck. It is almost unbearable.

There is a knock at the door. Since Wendy is dead, he opens the door without hesitation.

"Oh, Alexandra. Hi. How are you?" Eddy happily greets his neighbor. He is thankful for the escape from his thoughts.

"Good but exhausted," Alexandra says. "We just got back from our Ireland and Scotland trip. It takes me a while to get caught up with the time change thing. But you know all about that with your travels. I've been going through all the mail I had the maid put on the table. We got some of yours." She hands Eddy a stack of envelopes and postcards.

Eddy takes the pile and places it and his phone on the entry table. "Thanks. We do have a new postal carrier," he says.

"Well, she better get better fast. See you," Alexandra says and leaves before Eddy can answer.

"It's a he," Eddy mumbles as he closes the door. He has never been fond of Alexandra, but he wanted more conversation.

He is trying not to start thinking torturous thoughts again. Eddy slowly thumbs through the postcards. They are from people worldwide who he would have been clamoring to impress not so long ago. He finds it fascinating how the thought of these people makes him nauseous now.

Eddy scans the envelopes and then decides to get a nice bottle of wine from his private stash in his cellar. No one but Eddy is allowed downstairs. The real reason is that it is just a nasty basement. The illusion of having a fancy wine cellar is far greater than the reality, which is sometimes the case with many scenarios in higher social circles.

Lately, Eddy has been drinking mostly scotch and wants to treat himself to some excellent wine. He peruses his impressive collection of bottles in his drab, dank basement. Immediately out springs an inland taipan snake, striking his face multiple times from the shelf closest to his head.

Then a saw-scaled viper drops from the upper shelf to his shoulder and repeatedly bites Eddy's neck. He frantically tries to knock it off or catch it, but it rapidly delivers its venom and hangs onto his upper arm. Everything is happening so fast he is in shock! What is happening is worse than his greatest fears. Eddy battles but quickly becomes lightheaded and weak. He finds it hard to move as the bites continue. Twitching and paralysis begin to consume his body. He struggles up the stairs, trying to reach his phone on the entry table. He finally makes it, but his breathing all but stops. Eddy drops to the floor and labors a sigh.

Unbeknownst to Eddy, Wendy had managed to put some surprises in Eddy's cellar. She had made an impression mold of his front door key for access some time ago. When Eddy would go on a photography trip, she would sneak into his house and make sure there were no signs of other women having been there. It was easy to place the snakes and mice to sustain them, to lie in wait downstairs. The whole time Eddy created his safe room upstairs, Wendy had already set her trap in his basement. Knowing that offered Wendy some comfort as she painfully suffered and died.

~~~

Two days later, Officer Adams comes running into Garner's office. "The warrant took forever and the research even longer, but we got him. The night Winston was dropped off at the hospital, Eddy's car was there. Before that, the vehicle was at Monroe's cabin. He's toast. Good thing we didn't let on he was a suspect. You've got to love technology and GPS locators," Adams says excitedly.

Adams and Garner arrive at Eddy's house and knock on the door, with handcuffs in hand.

"You know, this guy's a real sick-o," Adams says.

"He's not sick. He's evil. Big difference," Garner replies.

They continue to knock but get no answer. "I'll call Eddy," Adams says.

Garner knocks again while Adams calls. They can hear Eddy's phone ringing inside the door. Garner and Adams look at each other. Without saying a word, Garner tries the door. It is unlocked and opens. They immediately see Eddy on the floor covered with countless bites and dried blood that oozed from each set of two punctures. Eddy's eyes are open, and he has a look of sheer panic on his face. He is a pale gray and undoubtedly dead.

"Out, out, close the door"! Garner shouts as they scramble outside. *"Call the guys with the boots."* Garner orders.

The two officers wait outside while the Hazardous Materials Unit searches the house. "Let's sit in the car. What if that thing or things, whatever it is, got outside!" Garner says. They sit in their patrol car, and Adams locks the doors. Garner laughs.

"What? You can't be too careful," Adams says, shrugging his shoulders.

"That's true," Garner replies. "It's a shame Eddy didn't think of that. Looks like his death was pretty gruesome. With some of those snake bites, you can be paralyzed but still alive and aware for hours."

"It's horrible," Adams says, shaking his head. "I'll be glad to get back to the old standard shooting and stabbing crimes. This whole thing has been majorly creepy. And evil."

Garner becomes very pensive and looks intently at Adams. "Evil is more real than most people ever fathom. In our work, sometimes we find that the boogeyman *is real*! And sometimes, the boogeyman is a woman."

"You're so right," Adams replies. "I don't know if I'll ever stop having nightmares."

Garner scratches his head. "By the way, my wife showed me in the Bible where God talks about the devil in Revelations. The devil *and* his evil companions are real, and she said God even *warned us*!"

"I didn't know that," Adams replies.

"I didn't either, but we should have. I bet a lot of people don't get it. My wife said that the devil—Satan and his evil cohorts just have to get a person started down a wrong path, and then they keep going by themselves. She said that Satan doesn't care if you're a little bad or a lot bad, as long as the bad part keeps you from being close to God. That's his main goal," Garner explains.

Adams is deep in thought. "So, the simple good versus evil is what it's all about?"

"Yep. That's it. We humans just complicate things."

"I bet all the people in prison constantly rehash how they went down the wrong path. But wait. If they do, then why is the recidivism rate so high?" Adams asks.

"That's easy. One—bad habits are hard to break. It's easier to start making wrong choices again. And two—there aren't enough good people offering a helping hand when people do need help. The devil has us right where he wants us, eh," Garner says.

"That's a lot to mull over," Adams admits.

"And I think it's a bit ironic. But if we had gotten here sooner, maybe something could have been done for Eddy, just like with Monroe. Timing always plays a part," Garner declares.

"Well, creepy Wevil got the last word after all," Adams says.

"I think it's more that she got the last strike," Garner smirks.

"Literally, eh," Adams shivers.

When Garner and Adams return to the station, they find that many cases can be closed with all the evidence and information that is now available on Wendy and Eddy. The entire department is ecstatic. The DA even says, "*Wow!*"

Epilogue

CONNECT

Gretchen and Chad do live *happily ever after*. A wooden heart covered with mustard seeds is over their bed , reminding them daily how blessed they are and how important it is to believe. They have two girls and a boy. Plus, they adopted another little boy. Gretchen had some complications and could only give birth to three, even though she tried hard for four as promised. Phyllis still grapples with that.

Phyllis is unsure exactly what to believe, but now she feels there must be something. Still, she does not believe in luck. So, Phyllis believes that Gretchen's grandmother had a hand in getting Chad and Gretchen together. She is perfectly content with that idea. If God is real, she loves the concept that He would care enough to listen to Gretchen's Gramma.

Auntie Phyllis, Uncle Hamer, and Grandpa Lloyd love and spoil the four children. All of them enjoy every moment together. Gretchen loves her family of choice and appreciates each of them more than most could ever imagine.

Chad and Gretchen create a successful summer camp for children from various states so that "kids can be kids." They experience all the fun nature, and the outdoors have to offer. Plus, they see and learn what real love looks like and should be for everyone.

Gretchen has forgiven her mother. However, she does not see her. She has forgiven her to be free of her childhood and her past. Forgiveness equals freedom, not necessarily an ongoing relationship. Her mother continues to drink and be involved with different men. That is certainly something Gretchen does not want her children subjected to ever. She wishes her mother well from a distance and hopes she will make changes for her own sake one day. However, that has no bearing on Gretchen's current wonderful life.

With all Gretchen has experienced, she has no doubt that God and Heaven are real! She also knows that Jesus does love her. Gretchen feels very blessed and so grateful every day.

Chad and Gretchen make a fantastic team. They pray together often and ask for guidance and direction to know who to help. Also, they believe in and ask for miracles, especially for others. They always give prayers of thanks and constantly rely on God's help.

Every night at bedtime, as a family, they hold hands and all sing "Jesus Loves Me." At the end of the song, they point to each other and say, "And He loves you, and you, and you…"

On the camp library wall, in big letters, it says:

Kindness & Goodness are a *choice.*
Choose today who and what you want to be. It is <u>your</u> choice.

~~~

Dreams *do* come true. Miracles *do* happen.
You just have to believe!

With faith the size of a grain of mustard seed,
you can move mountains.

see Matthew 17:20 KJV

~~~ Sometimes that mountain is *you!* ~~~

The Beginning
of a Wonderful Life and Love Story